THE ABOMINABLES

Praise for ONE DOG AND HIS BOY

SHORTLISTED
Galaxy 2011 Children's Book of the Year
Red House Children's Book Award

*"Children's book of the year... Eva Ibbotson is a writer
who understands a child's heart, which few others do... An
adventure to rival that other canine odyssey,*
The Hundred and One Dalmatians"
Amanda Craig, THE TIMES

*"Blows me away... It takes a sweetly old fashioned
story – boy wants dog – and makes it feel crispy,
new and even edgy"*
Frank Cottrell Boyce

"A storytelling and linguistic delight"
SCOTSMAN

*"Your next Christmas present to a child who
reads it will have to be a puppy"*
NEW STATESMAN

*"A lovely, funny, beautifully written story from
a cherished writer"*
DAILY MAIL

"An exquisitely crafted book with not a single wasted word"
SCHOOL ZONE – Librarian's Book Choice

Also by Eva Ibbotson

THE ABOMINABLES

Eva Ibbotson

Illustrated by Sharon Rentta

MARION LLOYD BOOKS

First published in the UK in 2012 by Marion Lloyd Books
An imprint of Scholastic Children's Books
Euston House, 24 Eversholt Street
London, NW1 1DB, UK
A division of Scholastic Ltd.
Registered office: Westfield Road, Southam, Warwickshire, CV47 0RA
SCHOLASTIC and associated logos are trademarks and/or registered trademarks of
Scholastic Inc.

ISBN 978 1407 13297 6

A CIP catalogue record for this book is available from the British Library

Printed by CPI Group (UK) Ltd, Croydon, CR0 4YY
Papers used by Scholastic Children's Books are
made from wood grown in sustainable forests.

3 5 7 9 10 8 6 4 2

www.scholastic.co.uk/zone

Contents

1

Kidnap

About a hundred years ago something dreadful happened in the mountains near Tibet.

A beautiful young girl called Lady Agatha Farlingham was sleeping peacefully in a tent pitched on a ledge below the summit of a mountain known as Nanvi Dar. Beside her, wearing a green woolly nightcap against the bitter cold, slept her father, the Earl of Farley, and in another tent close by slept their three porters, tough natives of the Himalayas, who carried their baggage and looked after them.

The Earl had come to the roof of the world to search for rare and unknown plants which grew only in these high and dangerous places. He was a famous plant hunter and he liked his daughter Agatha too much to leave her at home in England doing all the boring things that girls had to do in those days, like painting pictures of ruins, or taking walks with their governess, or visiting the poor, who often preferred to be left alone.

Soon after midnight on that awful night, Lady Agatha was woken by a most strange and unearthly sound – an eerie and mournful noise like a train with indigestion.

She sat up, pulled her father's heavy tweed jacket around her shoulders and bravely stepped outside. And then it happened. Out of the blackness and the snow there loomed a ghastly, gigantic, hairy THING. Before she could even scream, a pair of huge brown arms grasped the terrified girl and then the foul beast turned and, leaping swiftly back up the sheer side of the mountain, vanished out of sight.

The poor Earl and his porters searched and searched for many days, risking death in the cruel blizzards and the raging wind, but it was useless. The fresh snow had wiped out all possible tracks.

Only a blue
bedsock, kicked off by
the struggling girl, remained to Lady
Agatha's distraught father. He took it back to
England, to his ancestral home at Farley Towers,
and slept with it under his pillow for the rest of
his life. And when people asked him what had
happened to his lovely daughter, he always said
she must have lost her memory and wandered
away and been buried by an avalanche. Because he
simply wouldn't believe what all the porters told
him: that his daughter had been carried away by a
yeti – that vile monster who can tear a human being
limb from limb, or crunch one up in a single bite. A
creature so terrible and fearsome that it is known as
The Abominable Snowman.

But of course the porters were right. Agatha *had*
been carried away by a yeti. He had run with her
high over the sacred mountain of Nanvi Dar, and all

her kicks and struggles and screams felt no more to his brute strength than the hiccuping of a flea. Until at last the thin air, the bitter cold and blind terror brought release and the poor girl mercifully fainted.

When she came round she knew at once where she was. There could only be one place as beautiful as this: heaven. The sky above her head was a marvellous rich, royal blue with little fleecy clouds. The grass on which she lay was soft and sweet-smelling and studded with beautiful flowers: tiny blue gentians, golden primulas, scarlet lilies. Agatha sat up. She felt sore and bruised but that was understandable. You couldn't die and go to heaven without feeling a little bit uncomfortable.

She looked around. The air was warm, and she saw trees covered in red and white and cream blossoms as big as plates. There was a stream, crystal clear and bubbly, with kingfishers darting about its banks. Far above her an eagle circled lazily. She was in a broad valley, surrounded on every side by sheer, jagged cliffs and escarpments. And then to her surprise, beyond the steep ridges which surrounded the valley, she saw the unmistakable outline of the peak of Nanvi Dar, glittering white in the early morning sun.

"Perhaps I haven't died after all," said Lady Agatha.

And there was something else that didn't go with the idea of heaven in the least. A few metres away from her, sitting so quietly that she had taken it for a boulder or the stump of a huge tree, was an absolutely enormous dark brown beast. It wasn't a bear; it was much, much bigger than a bear. It wasn't a man; it was much, much hairier than any man. And then she remembered. A yeti. She had been carried away by a yeti over mountains so dangerous that she could never make her way back alone. She was trapped here in this secret valley, perhaps for ever.

"I should feel terribly frightened," thought Agatha.

But feeling frightened is an odd thing. You either feel it or you don't, and Agatha didn't. Instead she got up and walked quietly towards the yeti. Then she leaned forward and put her hand on the yeti's arm. At once she was buried up to the elbow in long, cool, silky, tickly hair, masses and masses of it.

The yeti leaned forward. He blew softly with his lower lip to clear away his hair – and then Lady Agatha Farlingham became the first human ever to see a yeti's face.

She thought it a most interesting and distinguished face. Yetis have huge, round, intelligent eyes as big as saucers. If you stop and look into a yeti's eyes, instead of just running away and screaming, you can't be afraid. Yetis also have snub noses and big ears and the ears have a most useful flap on them, an ear *lid*, which they can close. This saves them from getting earache in the fierce Himalayan winds, and is also useful when they don't want to hear what people are saying. Their mouths are big and generous-looking.

Best of all are their smiles. "Before I had seen a yeti smile," Lady Agatha used to say, "I didn't know what a smile was." Not only was the yeti's smile beautiful, it was very, very comforting to anyone who might be worrying about being eaten. If you want to know what a person eats, look at his teeth. The yeti's teeth were white and even and quite flat, like the teeth of a very clean sheep, and Agatha understood immediately not only that the yeti *wouldn't* eat her but that he *couldn't* eat her. And in fact, as she found out later, yetis are the strictest and most careful vegetarians.

"Oh, I *like* you," said Agatha, holding out her hand.

A great burden seemed to fall off the yeti's back. He got up and stood there, waiting, with his head on one side, till Agatha got up too, and then he began to lead her along the floor of the valley towards a little copse of slender Himalayan birches where some yaks were peacefully grazing. And as he walked, Agatha saw that his enormous feet – each about the size of a well-fed dachshund – had eight toes and were put on back to front. And this, of course, was why later when people tried to track yetis in the snow they never found them. Yetis who seem to be going are really coming, and yetis who seem to be coming are really going. It is as simple as that.

Suddenly the yeti stopped, bent down to a little hollow by the bank of the stream and began to clear away the dried grass and sticks which covered it. When he had finished he grunted in a pleased sort of way and then he moved aside so that Agatha could see what he had uncovered.

"Oh!" said Agatha. Sleeping peacefully, curled up in each other's arms, were two fat, furry baby yetis. She bent down to touch the one nearest to her. Its silly, big feet were pulled round its plump stomach and when it opened its eyes and looked at her, they were a deep and lovely blue.

Then she tickled the other yeti and it twitched in its sleep and woke too, and *its* eyes were a rich and serious brown.

But the yeti father had begun to look anxious.

Something wasn't right. He began to stir the babies round, prodding and digging and turning them over like underdone sausages. And then he pounced, and with a proud grunt, held something out to Agatha.

It was another baby yeti – but so small and squashed and funny-looking that it might just as well have been an old glove or a tea cosy or a run-over cat. And when it opened its eyes and looked at her, Agatha got a shock. One of its eyes was a bright and piercing blue, the other was a deep and serious brown.

"A wall-eyed yeti," said Agatha in amazement.

Later she called him Ambrose.

2

The Trouble with Yetis

As soon as she saw the orphaned yetis, Agatha gave up all idea of escaping from the secret valley. No, she would stay and bring the babies up to be God-fearing creatures and give them a mother's love. For she realized at once that the big yeti who had kidnapped her must be a widower who had lost his wife in some tragic accident and that he wanted her to care for his children.

And care for them she did. The very fat, blue-eyed baby was a girl and Agatha called her Lucy, after the kennelmaid who had been her best friend at Farley Towers. The brown-eyed yeti, who was a boy, she called Clarence. And of course there was Ambrose, with his mad eyes and his squashed face – Ambrose who was always being sat on by the others, or falling into mouse-hare holes, or getting lost.

The first thing Agatha did, naturally, was to teach all the yetis to talk. Father learnt to speak quite quickly even though he was over three hundred years old by the time Agatha came to the valley and it is not so easy to learn things as you get older. And of course the children learnt as easily as they breathed.

After that, Agatha taught them all the things that her governess had taught her, like the importance of good manners: not burping after meals, not scratching under the armpits however much one itched, and *never* closing one's ear lids when people were speaking to one. She taught them how to clean between their teeth with a sharpened stick, and how to wash their eight-toed, backward-pointing feet in the stream after they'd been running because smelly feet are *not* polite. She taught them sums and their alphabet and how to sing hymns. Best of all, she used to tell them stories. Soon after she arrived in the valley, Father had realized that a well-bred English girl needed somewhere to call home, and he had gathered stones and built her a little house, no more than a hut really, roofing it with branches and grass. In the evenings, Agatha would sit outside with the yetis around her. "Once upon a time..." she would begin.

The yetis were *mad* about stories. *Puss in Boots*, *Jack and the Beanstalk*, *The Three Bears* – all day they followed her about, begging for more. As for Ambrose, long before dawn Agatha could hear him sitting and *breathing* outside the entrance to her hut (by the time he was two years old he was much too big to get through it), waiting and waiting to hear about Ali Baba, or poor Cinderella, or Dick Whittington's cat.

At first Lady Agatha was surprised by how easily the yetis took to a civilized English upbringing, but she soon realized that they were truly kind and considerate by nature, not only to each other, but to every living thing. In the mornings, when she combed them, they would cup their huge hands to catch the little spiders and beetles that had crept into their hair during the night, and release them carefully on to the ground. They always looked where they were putting their huge feet, avoiding worm casts and spiders' nests and molehills, in case someone was at home. So they were particularly pleased when Agatha taught them to say sorry, for you should Always Apologize for Any Inconvenience You Have Caused.

But when they began to apologize to everything they ate (and yetis eat a lot), saying "Sorry, mango," "Sorry, flower," "Sorry, yak-milk pancake," Lady Agatha thought that this was going too far – Moderation In All Things – and taught them to say grace. "For what we are about to receive may the Lord make us truly thankful." It was not a great improvement. They did say grace politely when they sat down to a meal together. But yetis graze quite a lot, on grass or fruit or young tree shoots, and they went on apologizing as they wandered about, so that there was an almost constant murmuring in the hidden valley, rather like a swarm of contented bees. Agatha tried to persuade them that saying sorry to every nut and berry was not the English Way, but although she was a remarkably good governess, in this she failed. The yetis continued to apologize to every blade of grass.

This doesn't mean, of course, that they were perfect. Perfect yetis, like perfect people, would have been dull. Lucy's little problem was food. She really loved eating. All day one could hear Lucy wandering up and down the valley saying, "Sorry," before she cropped a mouthful of grass or, "Sorry, tree," before she chewed up a branch. The result of this, of course, was that she became very fat, and the hair on her stomach looked as though it was growing on an enormous kettledrum. And because her stomach was always full, Lucy slept badly. Or rather she *slept* all right but she walked in her sleep. When you heard a terrible crash or a fearful rumbling noise in the mountains of Nanvi Dar, it wasn't necessarily a rock fall or an avalanche. It was just as likely to be Lucy falling over a tree stump as she blundered with unseeing eyes out of her bed.

Clarence had a problem too. With him it was his brain. When he was small, Clarence had been naughty and left the valley without telling Lady Agatha and gone climbing on his own, and a gigantic boulder had come loose and hit him on the head. After that Clarence's brain did not work too well, so that while he was as strong as the others and could pick a fir-tree as easily as a daisy, he was really not very bright and could only say one word at a time and that was usually wrong.

As for Ambrose, he started life as a little mewling thing, all eyes and feet and not much in between, and Agatha had some very worrying moments, sitting up with him when he was teething or running a temperature. Once, when he had had a runny nose for a full month, she said, half-joking, "Ambrose, you really are an abominable snowman." The name stuck and he was Ambrose the Abominable from then on. Because of all the trouble he had caused her as a baby, and the times when she seriously thought he might not survive, he had a special place in Agatha's heart. This sometimes happens to mothers, however hard they try to love all their children absolutely equally. But at last the worst was over, and Ambrose grew fast, and he grew strong. When he was nineteen, before he lost his milk teeth, he pushed over the biggest pine tree in the valley looking for woodlice to play with, and he would cheerfully lift boulders the size of telephone boxes to help Lucy make a Wendy house. If anyone had happened to catch sight of Ambrose, with his wall-eye and enormous strength, their knees would have started to tremble and sweat would have broken out on their brow. He really did look like people imagined yetis to be –

abominable. In actual fact, however, he was the soppiest yeti ever, forever making daisy chains for Lady Agatha, or lying beside her asking if there were fairies in the stars, or begging for another story. He always gave things away – food to Lucy, or pretty stones to Clarence, and sometimes Lady Agatha thought it might be a good thing if he really was a tiny little bit abominable. She would never have called him wet, exactly, or soft (he never complained when he hurt himself), but was he just a little bit too kind for his own good?

When Agatha had been in the valley about thirty years and Ambrose, Clarence and Lucy were already children rather than babies, a very old and stringy female yeti tottered into the valley from a range of mountains to the east. They called her Grandma, and just sometimes after she had taught her to speak, Agatha wished she hadn't, because all Grandma did was grumble. She grumbled about her rheumatism, she grumbled about her teeth. She grumbled about her share of juniper berries at lunchtime and about how careless Ambrose was, bouncing on her corns. But the yetis knew one had to be kind and gentle to the old and they behaved beautifully to Grandma. The only thing they wouldn't do, even for Lady Agatha, was to keep their ear lids open when she sang. And really, you couldn't blame them. Grandma singing "Onward Christian Soldiers" as she milked the yaks didn't just sound like a road drill. It sounded like a road drill with tonsillitis.

Even after Grandma came, Agatha's family was not complete. A few years later, Father, who sometimes went exploring in the High Places, came back with a rather shy and nervous yeti a few years younger than himself.

When he was young, Uncle Otto (as they called him) had had a Dreadful Experience. He was standing on a pinnacle of rock admiring a most beautiful and uplifting sunrise, when two Sherpa porters, carrying the baggage for a party of mountaineers, had come round the corner and seen him. Uncle Otto had smiled most politely, showing all his beautiful white teeth in welcome, but the porters had just screamed and gibbered and, throwing down their packs, had rushed down the mountain so fast that one of them had fallen into a crevasse and been killed.

After this, Uncle Otto had always felt shy and unwanted, and soon afterwards a bald patch had appeared on his high, domed forehead. There is nothing like worry for making your hair fall out. But when Agatha taught him to speak, and to read, she was amazed at his intelligence. In the pocket of her father's jacket, which she had slipped on before she was carried away, had been a copy of the Bible, and Uncle Otto used to spend hours sitting under his favourite rhododendron tree and reading. What's more he never skipped like the others did but even read the bits where Ahaz begat Jehoadah and Jehoadah begat Alameth. Not that he was conceited – far from it. It was the others who were so proud of him.

And so the years passed peacefully and happily for Agatha and her yetis in the secret valley of Nanvi Dar. Because there was no smoke to get into her lungs, or petrol fumes to give her headaches, or chemicals to mess up her food, Agatha grew old only very, very slowly. Nearly a hundred years after she had come to the valley she was still healthy and strong.

But in the meantime the world outside was changing. More and more mountaineers came to climb the high peaks with newer and shinier tents and ropes and ice axes and stood about on the top of them being photographed and quarrelling about who had got there first. And then one day Clarence said, "'ook! 'ook!" and when they had looked up to where he was pointing they saw, far away, a strange red bird in the sky – a helicopter – which quite amazed Lady Agatha, who'd left England when there weren't even any motor cars.

After that came the hotel.

It was a huge, luxury hotel – the Hotel Himalaya, they called it

— built just across the border in the province of Bukhim, so that wealthy people who were too lazy to walk anywhere could sit in their rooms and watch the sun go down on the peaks of Nanvi Dar. The hotel meant new roads, and plane loads of tourists. It meant litter on the snowy slopes, and monasteries serving egg and chips and rubbishy souvenirs. It also meant new kinds of people: property developers and speculators, people who thought of the mountains not as beautiful places to be respected but as something that might make them rich.

Lady Agatha wasn't a worrier, but she began to worry now. It seemed to her only a matter of time before someone discovered the valley. And she knew enough about the cruel and terrible things that might happen to her yetis if the wrong people found them. They could be put in zoos behind bars with people poking them with umbrellas and throwing toffee papers into their cages. They could be put in a circus or a funfair and treated like freaks. Or – but this was so awful that Agatha began to shiver even as

19

she thought of it – they could be hunted and killed for sport as the great mammals of Africa had been hunted and killed when man first set eyes on them.

"Now listen, my dears," she said to her yetis, gathering them around her. "I must ask you to stay safely hidden in the valley. No climbing in the High Places. No exploring."

"But I want to meet humans," said Ambrose. "You're a human. They could be our friends and tell us stories, like you do. And we could help them lift things."

Lady Agatha sighed. She blamed herself, of course, for not having been more honest about the world from which she came. But how could she explain about human wickedness to the yetis? They would simply never understand it. She could only hope that the yetis would obey her.

And the yetis did. Ambrose, in any case, was busy taming his pet yak, an animal called Hubert. Yaks (which are a sort of small and very shaggy cow) are stubborn and hardy animals. But they are not very clever at the best of times. They don't need to be because all they do is eat grass at one end and give milk at the other. All the same, there had probably never before been a yak as stupid as Hubert.

He was about the size of a folding pram, with

a sad, boot-shaped face, a crumpled left horn and knees which knocked together when he walked. Hubert knew he had a mother, but he was never quite sure which of the yaks was her, and when he did find her he would suddenly get the idea that he was supposed to be back with Ambrose. Sometimes he would get so muddled that he would just bury his head in a hollow tree or a hole in the ground and give up; there were Hubert Holes like that all over the valley. Ambrose, however, wouldn't hear a word against him, and as he said, Hubert was probably the only potholing yak in the world.

But though all the yetis were as good and careful as could be, something dreadful did happen after all.

In a way it was Lady Agatha's fault for cooking such a lovely yak-milk pudding for their supper. Father and Uncle Otto had three helpings each; Grandma and Clarence and Ambrose had two. But Lucy said, "May the Lord make us truly thankful," to the yak-milk pudding no less than *five* times. Nobody can have five helpings of pudding and sleep soundly. And that night, Lucy rose from the bed of leaves in which she slept beside her brothers, and with her blue eyes wide open and her arms stretched out in front of her she walked – sightless and fast asleep – across the meadows, scaled apparently without effort the ferocious cliffs surrounding the valley, and stepped out on to the eternal snows.

3

Footprints in the Snow

Lucy got back safely to the valley – sleepwalkers usually seem to get back to their beds. But the glacier she had walked across had just had a new fall of snow. And right across it, from end to end, she left a row of footprints. Huge, clear, dachshund-sized prints: eight toes, rounded heels and all. There is nothing like a portly yeti with flat feet for making marks which even a nitwit could identify.

If only it had snowed, then things might have gone on as before. But it didn't snow, not the next day or the next. And on the third day a couple of climbers came across the prints.

Within a week photographs of Lucy's footprints were on the front page of newspapers all over the world. All the old stories about Abominable Snowmen were dragged out again: how fierce they were, how huge... How they could swallow three goats at a gulp, how just to *see* one was to die within the week.

The owners of the Hotel Himalaya, who knew all about how to make money, set to work at once. The day after the climbers had burst breathlessly into

the hotel dining room with their news, people were sent out to find the footprints and preserve them, by roping them off, putting up signs, and covering them with tarpaulins in case it snowed. And a few days later full-page advertisements appeared in all the travel magazines and brochures, saying, *Enjoy the Experience of a Lifetime! A week at the luxury Hotel Himalaya with guided Yeti Safari to the famous footprints!* And underneath a picture of a hairy monster with fangs and blood dripping down its chin were the words *Who will be the first to meet the Abominable Snowman Face to Face? IT COULD BE YOU!*

But it wasn't a photographer or a journalist or a thrill-seeking tourist who found the secret valley of Nanvi Dar. It was a boy; quite a young one. And his name was Con.

Con was a pageboy at the Hotel Himalaya in Bukhim. He was, perhaps, the smallest pageboy in the world and in Britain he would not have been allowed to work at all because he was far too young.

When Con's father, who ran a restaurant in London, had been offered the job of chef in the new hotel in Bukhim, he had tried to leave Con and his sister Ellen behind at nice boarding schools in England. But Con had dug in his heels. He was not, he said, going to spend his time rushing about on cricket pitches in silly white pants, or letting idiot boys hit him on the head with pillows in the dorm, when he could be living in one of the most exciting places in the world.

"And anyway," he'd said to his father, "I might see a yeti."

Con's father didn't believe in yetis but he believed in Con. And when Con and Ellen both promised to work very hard at their lessons, he agreed to take them along.

And the children kept their promise, and worked very hard indeed. Even so, because they didn't have to stand about in Assembly having headmasters make speeches to them, or hang around in draughty schoolyards waiting for whistles to blow, or fight for their school dinners, they had lots of spare time. So in the afternoons Con put on a red uniform with silver buttons and helped to look after the visitors, and Ellen, who was very domesticated and liked to be busy, worked with the maids. The children's mother had been killed in a car crash two years earlier and it helped Ellen to do the things she'd done with her.

When Con had told his father that he might see a yeti he hadn't been joking. Ever since he'd first read about yetis, he'd had a special feeling about them. When people had scoffed and said there weren't any such things, Con had just shrugged. He just *knew* there were and that one day he would see one.

So when Lucy's footsteps had first been seen on the slopes of Nanvi Dar, Con had been incredibly happy and excited. He longed to join the parties of visitors on the trek up to the glacier. For the Yeti Safari was a huge success. People arrived at the Hotel Himalaya from all over the world. But soon Con stopped being happy and began to feel quite sick. The hotel manager did everything he could to cash in on the yetis, selling yeti pyjama cases and yeti headscarves and yeti postcards which made them look like dim-witted baboons. And finally, when Con had spent some time helping groups of tourists get ready for their trek, running backwards and forwards with Thermos flasks they had left in their rooms, tying their bootlaces, polishing their snow goggles, pulling on their padded mittens and smearing suncream on their noses, he stopped feeling sick and began to be frightened.

In one of the parties there was a couple of beetroot-faced army officers drinking rum out of silver hip flasks who talked about "getting a potshot at the brutes, eh?" In another there was a very thin woman wearing boots which Con was absolutely sure were made from the skin of the terribly rare snow leopard. She kept laughing like a hyena and telling her husband that she "*must* have a yeti-skin coat, daah-ling". When a third group departed which included a fat little man who seemed to think a yeti was a kind of elephant because he did nothing except wonder how much one could get for a pair of tusks, Con had had enough.

That night he couldn't get to sleep. He was just too horribly angry. He knew what would happen if one of those rich, bored, stupid people really did stumble across a yeti. Nobody who cared deeply about those mysterious creatures could even afford to buy a cup of tea in the Hotel Himalaya, let alone go on the ridiculously expensive Yeti Safari. So it was only a question of time.

"I wish they had never found those footprints," he said to himself. And then he knew what he had to do.

He woke an hour before dawn, dressed quickly in the warmest things he had and began carefully and methodically to pack his rucksack. He had been out hiking many times, and knew what he would need. But he also knew that he was planning something very dangerous, and probably very foolish. He left a note for Ellen and his father. Then he slipped out of the hotel.

The route up to the glacier was not hard to follow. It had been well trampled the last few weeks, there were fixed ropes at the more difficult places, and it was certainly no harder for Con than for the little fat man. He reckoned on cutting the time the guided parties took by several hours, because they moved very slowly, with frequent stops for tea and titbits. And in the early afternoon they stopped at a specially prepared campsite with fires blazing and servants rushing about with hot meals and drinks. Even so, Con was expecting to spend at least one night well above the treeline at a dangerously high altitude.

By mid-afternoon, exhausted and breathing with difficulty in the thin air, Con was standing on the glacier in the shadow of the huge, towering rock face which made up the eastern shoulder of Nanvi Dar. It was easy to find the footprints. Already hundreds of tourists had shuffled around them. But now it was over. When he was finished, the mountains and their secret inhabitants could find peace again.

He had to hurry. If he did not get off the glacier and find some kind of shelter before nightfall then he would die, no doubt about it. All he needed to do was remove the protective covering, and let the snow clouds which were gathering in the west do the rest. He pulled the heavy tarpaulins aside and then, to be absolutely sure, he started kicking snow into the prints, tramping in them, so that they were completely obliterated. He followed the prints, kicking and stamping, all the way to where the snow of the glacier ended and the footprints (if you followed them the right way, letting the *heels* lead you) stopped. Over this great cliff of rock the yeti must have clambered, but a human being could not hope to follow. No less than three mountaineering expeditions, with the newest equipment, had tried to conquer the eastern ramparts of Nanvi Dar and failed.

Afterwards, Grandma said it was the will of God, because why should Con have come to the sheer rock face just at that moment? The moment when there burst out of the space between two boulders at the base of the cliff a most extraordinary THING.

A sort of molehill it seemed to be. But were molehills hairy? And did they *bleat*?

Completely puzzled, Con scrambled up to have a closer look.

The THING was a head. The small, earth-covered head of a very worried baby yak.

Hubert had had a dreadful day. First he'd gone up to someone who he was absolutely certain was his mother but she hadn't been, and had been rude about it. Then he'd trotted back to find Ambrose but Ambrose was helping Lady Agatha to pick bamboo shoots and he wasn't there. By this time Hubert was so muddled that he'd gone and buried his head in a hole, meaning to wait till things got clearer inside his

head. But the hole hadn't been like his usual holes. It had gone on and on and on. And now he had come out in this strange place and his back end was stuck in the mountain and it was all very difficult and very hopeless and very sad.

"Don't worry, little Bootface," said Con, patting the yak on the nose, "I'll soon get you clear."

He took hold of Hubert's shoulders and began tugging and pulling – carefully but with all his strength. For a while nothing happened except that Hubert's bleats got more and more frantic. Then suddenly there was a popping noise and in a shower of small stones, Hubert's backside came out of the mountain and fell across Con's feet.

"A *tunnel*?" said Con, peering across Hubert into the deep, black hole from which the yak had come. "It can't be!"

But it was: a narrow channel through the side of the mountain which had once been the bed of an underground river.

"You must have come from the other side," said Con wonderingly. "And if I lie down I'm smaller than you are..."

He dropped on to his hands and knees and began to edge his way into the tunnel. The sunshine turned to grey twilight, then to darkness: pitch darkness as

Hubert, terrified of being left alone, turned back and followed him.

It was a fearful journey and agonizingly slow. Water trickled down the sides of the rock, jagged daggers of ice hung from the roof; Con had never been so cold. Often he wanted to stop and go back but behind him, blocking off all retreat, puffing, dribbling, butting with his crumpled horn – came Hubert.

"I ... can't do it," gasped Con. The passage was getting narrower now. It was like being in an endless, ice-cold grave. "I can't..."

And then he saw it. A narrow chink of light. Golden light. *Sunlight.*

The chink grew bigger. It had grass in it; flowers; the flash of water... And something else...

"No," breathed Con, "I don't believe it."

But it was true. On a tussock of grass sat a little old lady wearing a long, white flannel nightdress. Beside her, his armchair-sized head within reach of her hand, lay an enormous chocolate-coloured creature whose left ear she was gently scratching. Another huge beast – with a dreamy look and the largest stomach Con had ever seen – was sitting nearby, peacefully combing out her elbows. Three more of them were paddling in the stream or picking flowers and one – his bald patch gleaming in the sunlight – was leaning against a tree and reading a book.

"Tell it again," came the voice of the chocolate-coloured yeti. "Tell where the Ugly Sisters tried to cut off their toes to get them in the glass slipper?"

"That's enough for today." The old lady's voice was firm. The creature lifted his head and began reluctantly to get up. Then he let out a great yell.

"Look, Lady Agatha! Look, everybody! It's a funny sort of human dwarf thing. And it's come out of Hubert's hole!"

4

A Plan

An hour later, as the shadows lengthened and the sun began to set behind the eastern escarpments of the secret valley, Con was sitting on a grassy bank beside the stream, drinking the warm yak's milk that Lady Agatha had heated for him on a charcoal fire.

"So it's the crater of an extinct volcano?"

"Well so I believe," said Lady Agatha. "There are some marvellous hot springs over there. I don't know what I would have done without hot water when the children were small. And the soil is wonderfully fertile, even better than Hampshire. But are you sure," Lady Agatha broke off, "that your father won't be worried about you?"

"Well, I did leave a note," said Con, "so he won't be *too* worried until tomorrow evening. Anyway," he went on contentedly, "I can't leave tonight, can I?"

All around him sat the yetis, as close to him as they could get, but trying very hard not to stare because they knew it was rude.

"I don't *mind* him having no hair on his face," whispered Ambrose to his sister. "I just know we are going to be friends."

35

"He's very *thin*," murmured Lucy worriedly. "Shall I go and say sorry to some grass for him?"

"Now run along, all of you," said Lady Agatha, when Con had finished drinking. "I want to talk to this boy alone before bedtime."

"But he hasn't told me a *story*," wailed Ambrose.

"He knows a new one, about a chicken called Donald!"

"Not a chicken, Ambrose," said Con. "A duck."

"Later, dear," said Lady Agatha, and Ambrose ambled off after the others to investigate Hubert's hole, which had turned out to be a tunnel to the world outside.

When they had gone, Lady Agatha looked at

Con's serious, thoughtful face, and sighed.

"If you'd been grown up," she said, "not still a child, I'd have thought you'd been sent in answer to my prayers."

Con was sitting on the grass at her feet, his hands round his knees.

"Why?" he said.

For a moment she didn't answer. Then she said: "For some time now, I have thought that my yetis ought to leave the valley. That they ought to be taken to a place where they will be absolutely safe. I am an extremely old woman, you see. How old you might not believe. And if anyone found them here in the wilds after my death ... well, anything could happen."

Con was silent. He knew only too well how right she was. Those dreadful people in the hotel...

"Father would always be safe," Lady Agatha went on. "He knows every rock, every crevasse; he's wise and he can be cunning. But the children ... they're so trusting. And Grandma is old, and Uncle Otto ... well, he's a scholar and they're never very good at looking after themselves."

"But where would they go, Lady Agatha? Where would you take them?"

A dreamy look came into her face. "To my old

home. To Farley Towers, in Hampshire."

"All the way to Britain!" Con was amazed. It was a journey half across the world, through the burning plains of India, the stony wastes of Afghanistan, across Iran and Turkey, and almost the whole length of Europe. How could the yetis ever manage that?

"It's such a beautiful place, Farley. Soft, mellow brick terraces with peacocks, a deer park, a lake... My Little Ones would be safe there, I know, and it's just the life for them. Drawing Room Tea, Church on Sundays, Croquet..."

"But, Lady Agatha, it's years since you left. Anything could have happened to Farley Towers."

But Lady Agatha said she was certain that her old home was just as she had left it and still in the charge of some dear member of her family who would welcome and care for the yetis just as she had done. "After all," she said, "An Englishman's Home is Still His Castle."

Con was beginning to understand. "Was that why you wanted me to be grown up? So that I could help you to take your yetis to England?"

"So that you could take them *for* me. I'm far too old to travel. I shall die here in this valley where I have lived so happily."

Con's mind was racing ahead, thinking out the

yetis' journey.

"It would have to be a secret, I suppose?"

"Indeed, yes," said Lady Agatha. "The *strictest* secret. It would be most dangerous if anyone came upon them before they were safe at Farley Towers."

Con was silent, his forehead furrowed. "Do yetis hibernate?" he said at last. "Go to sleep through the winter, I mean, like bears?"

"Not hibernate, exactly," said Lady Agatha, "but in severe weather conditions with extreme cold they can go into a sort of coma. Their heartbeat slows down, and they don't need food or drink. They can survive almost anything. No yeti has ever died of exposure."

"Well, in that case," said Con, "I think I can see how to get them to England without anyone knowing."

And he told her his plan. Once a week, said Con, huge, refrigerated lorries came all the way from Britain to the Hotel Himalaya, bringing frozen meat for the visitors who were too picky to try the local delicacies – sour cheese smoked in yak dung, or tea with rancid butter floating in it. Usually these lorries returned with a load of spices, or cloth, or goatskins which the Bukhimese wanted to sell in Britain. "But just once," said Con, "if I can square it with the driver, I reckon it could return with yetis."

Lady Agatha stared at him. Then: "I have something which might help to persuade the driver," she said.

She disappeared into her stone hut and came back with a little bag made out of the hem of her flannel nightdress. "Open it!" she commanded.

Con took the bag, which was surprisingly heavy, and undid the string. The metal inside, catching the sunlight, was unmistakable.

"Gold," he said, wonderingly.

"I dredged it up from the river," said Lady Agatha. "It's silly stuff but I thought it might come in useful. I need hardly tell you that no one must ever know where it came from." She closed the bag and sat down again on her tussock. "There's one thing you've forgotten," she said. "Where would you hide the yetis till the lorry came?"

Con grinned. "In the last place that anyone would look for them. In the Bridal Suite of the hotel. It's a terribly grand set of rooms on the top floor, quite cut off from the rest of the hotel, with its own lift and everything. The Prince of Pettelsdorf booked it this week for his honeymoon but he's cancelled. My sister knows where the keys are; she'd help me smuggle them in."

Lady Agatha was silent. "It's quite impossible, of

course. Quite out of the question that I could let a child as young as you take on the responsibility of such a journey."

But Con wasn't so easily beaten. "How old were you when you came to the valley?" he asked innocently.

Lady Agatha blushed. "Older than you." There was a pause. "Well, not much older... Oh, dear, I don't know what to say."

"Then say yes," begged Con.

This time the pause seemed endless. "All right," said Lady Agatha at last. "You can take my yetis for me. I'll say it. Yes."

Over breakfast the next day Lady Agatha broke the news to the yetis, and they spent the rest of the morning crying.

When yetis cry, just as when they smile, they do not hold back. They do not sniffle or hiccup or gulp. They weep rivers.

Now they cried so hard that their fur became all dark and wet, so that they looked more like huge walruses or seals than Abominable Snowmen.

They cried because they were leaving Lady Agatha whom they loved so dearly, and the beautiful valley of Nanvi Dar where they had lived all their lives. They cried because they were leaving the trees and the birds and the flowers, and they cried because the yaks would be sad without them.

"I will be able to take Hubert?" Ambrose asked anxiously.

"Now, Ambrose," said Lady Agatha gently, "I've told you time and time again that this is going to be a difficult and dangerous journey. How do you think Con can take a yak? Especially a yak that doesn't even know its own mother."

So that of course started Ambrose off again. But when they had cried so much that there was hardly a tear left in any of them, the yetis secretly began to get rather excited about their journey.

"Tell us again about Farley Towers," Ambrose begged. And Lady Agatha closed her eyes and in a dreamy voice she told them about the great vine that grew on the south wall, about the yew trees clipped into the most beautiful shapes, about the big peaceful library with over five thousand books bound in rich, dark leather and the carved four-poster bed in which Queen Elizabeth had slept and in which Ambrose might be allowed to sleep too if only he was a good yeti and stopped *crying*.

While the yetis went up and down the valley saying, "Goodbye, juniper bush", "Goodbye, bird's nest", "Goodbye, beetles", Lady Agatha told Con some of the things she thought he ought to know, like what to do when Grandma's knees went under her and about Clarence not having a brain and about Lucy's sleepwalking. She told him that Uncle Otto liked having something rubbed into his bald patch once a day ("Anything will do," she said. "It's just to show you care") and that Ambrose, although he looked abominable, definitely was not – quite the opposite.

Above all she warned Con to be very careful because the yetis, though the gentlest of creatures, did not always know their own strength and could easily break someone's arm while just shaking hands with them. And she showed him some scars she had got in the early days before the yetis had understood that people were so frail and breakable.

Then she called all the yetis together and made a speech. She said how painful it was for her to part with them, but that she knew Con would be like a father to them and that they would be happy at Farley Towers. She reminded them how wrong it was to use Bad Language, or Forget To Do To Others As They Would Be Done By, and that they were to be sure to chew everything they ate thirty-two times so as not to get Lumps In The Stomach. "And now," she said, "I'm going to give each of you a present to take away."

"'esent," said Clarence excitedly. "'esent, 'esent!" He always seemed to understand things like that.

Lady Agatha turned and went into the little stone hut which had been her home since she first came to the valley. There she kept some of the things she had been wearing when Father carried her away and which were the only treasures she had.

"Grandma first," said Lady Agatha when she came out. And she gave Grandma the delicate, fleecy white shawl that had been round her shoulders when she slept.

Grandma really loved it. It was far too small to wrap around her shoulders, but she could use it as a headscarf and tie it under her chin. It was a crochet shawl with big open-work holes so that little tufts of grey and ginger hair sprouted out of the centre of each rosette, giving her a most distinguished look. To Uncle Otto she gave the woolly nightcap

she had been wearing when she was carried away. With a couple of hairpins, she fastened it with her own hands over Otto's bald patch – a most tactful present, because even if the bald patch *did* grow bigger, no one, now, would ever know.

For Lucy, Lady Agatha had kept a golden locket with a picture of Queen Victoria and all her nine children on it. She had made an extra long cord of plaited yak's hair for it and when Lucy put it on everybody agreed that nothing more beautiful than Queen Victoria and all her children nestling against the furry dome of Lucy's stomach had ever been seen in Nanvi Dar.

Clarence got the brass compass which had been in the pocket of the Earl's jacket. He wandered about with a blissful look on his face saying "'ick-'ock, 'ick-'ock," because he thought it was a watch. And from then on, whenever someone wanted to know the time, he always studied his compass with an important look on his face.

For Father, Lady Agatha had kept the Earl's cigar case. It was very valuable – pure gold studded with rubies – and there was a moment of silence as the yetis took in this costly present.

Father took it in his huge, gentle hands. He turned it over, admired the workmanship and the glitter of the rubies. Then he handed it back to Lady Agatha.

"I don't need a farewell present," he said in his deep, serious voice.

"But—"

"I don't need it," Father went on, "because I'm not going away."

Everyone looked at him, thunderstruck.

"Aren't you going with us, Father?" asked Ambrose in a trembly voice.

Father shook his head. "A hundred years ago I brought the Lady Farlingham to this valley. She cared for my children, she gave us speech, she taught us everything she knew. If I left her now to die alone, I should bring shame for ever to the name of yeti."

When he had finished there was a long and solemn silence. Then all the yetis slowly nodded their enormous heads. What Father had said was almost unbearably sad, but it was *right*.

"I'm not in the least afraid of dying," said Lady Agatha briskly. "After all, everyone enjoys going to sleep. So why not going to sleep for good?"

But nothing could shift Father. He said he was staying with her and anyone who wanted to move him from the valley was welcome to try. Since Father was far and away the strongest of all the yetis, that was the end of that.

But of course after that everybody began to cry again because Father was behaving so beautifully and because they would have to go without him and because Lady Agatha wasn't going to live for ever and ever, which was what Ambrose wanted her to do.

"Come, come," said Lady Agatha, though she was secretly very moved by Father's words, "this won't do. Ambrose hasn't had his present yet."

Ambrose's present was the most special one of all. It was one of the blue bedsocks that Lady Agatha had worn when she was carried away, and it still had a name tag inside saying: *Agatha Emily Farlingham, Farley Towers, Hants.*

"So when you arrive, Ambrose, and show them this sock, my family will know that you really come from me."

"It's like a sort of password," said Con.

Ambrose was incredibly pleased. He tried the sock on his foot but it would only cover about three of his eight enormous toes. Then he tried it on his left ear, but it kept slipping off. So Lady Agatha plaited a cord for him, like Lucy's, and he wore the bedsock across his chest like a medal.

And then the dreaded moment could be postponed no longer. The yetis kissed Lady Agatha over and over again, they hugged Father, and they cried and cried till Con thought they would never get away. But at last they were ready and with a stout stick to help Grandma they made their way to the head of the valley.

Con could have sworn that Ambrose simply didn't have any tears left. But just as he started the steep ascent up the scree, a last wail broke from him. "My yak! I never said goodbye to my yak!"

But Con knew that he had to be firm. "Look, Ambrose," he said, "you don't want to upset Hubert, do you? You know how sensitive he is."

"He'll think I don't love him," said Ambrose, and his brown eye, which felt things more than his blue one, began to fill up again.

But here the other yetis came to Con's rescue. "Now, Ambrose," said Grandma firmly, "you know that that animal hasn't had a thought in his head since the day he was born."

"And maybe when you're safe at Farley Towers you can send for him," said Con.

"Really?" said Ambrose.

"Really," said Con.

There was no more to say. They had come to the foot of the towering cliff wall that had protected the secret valley for thousands of years. Otto picked up Con, tucked him under his arm, and began swarming up the unclimbable rock face like an enormous hairy spider.

And then one by one the yetis filed in behind him and left for ever the lovely valley of Nanvi Dar.

5

The Bridal Suite

For Con the journey across the High Peaks was a dreadful one. As darkness fell they came across the eastern shoulder of Nanvi Dar, and though Con rode on Uncle Otto's shoulders, the thin air and the biting wind were almost more than he could bear. For the yetis, of course, it was not much worse than an evening stroll, even though they were at times wading through waist-high snow, leaping over crevasses or scrambling down hair-raising icefalls. Con burrowed as deep as he could into Uncle Otto's thick coat, and gritted his teeth.

Ambrose on the other hand had recovered from his sorrow about Hubert, and was in high spirits.

"Will there be proper beds, like in 'The Princess and the Pea'? What's a suite … is it sweet like fruit, or sweet like baby squirrels?" Con was too stiff and frozen to answer.

But at last they were below the snowline and walking down a broad river valley, sheltered from the wind. Scrub and grassland gave way to majestic cedars and pines, and the lights of the hotel appeared shining through the trees.

"Oh, oh, oh," said Ambrose, "it's like in a story!"

Otto lifted Con from his shoulders, and placed him carefully on the ground.

"We will have to be very quiet," said Con. "You must wait outside, and stay out of sight until I have been in and talked to my sister." Then he went on alone.

Ellen wasn't really asleep. She had been a bit worried the night before, in spite of Con's note. Now it was the middle of the second night, and she knew that in the morning she must raise the alarm and start expecting the worst.

So when her door opened silently and Con crept in she was up in an instant.

"Thank goodness you're back, I was getting really scared."

"I'm fine. Just be quiet and listen to me."

Con explained.

Some people, if they were told in the middle of the night that there were five Abominable Snowmen outside who needed to be smuggled into the bridal suite of a luxury hotel, might have asked a lot of questions, or made a fuss. But Ellen was not some people.

"I'll get the keys and wait for you up there," said Ellen. "Are yetis very big?"

Con said yes he could honestly say that they were on the large side.

"Then they'll have to come up one by one. It's going to take a while. We'll wait for you up there." And Ellen pulled on a dressing gown and went to get the keys. Con went back outside.

Yetis are absolute experts at being quiet. In the moonlight, five great shadows flitted across the perfectly mown lawn towards the hotel. The only sound was an almost inaudible "sorry" from Lucy, who was feeling peckish after her walk and happened to pass a bed of Himalayan poppies.

"Right," whispered Con, "Grandma can come first." And while the others made themselves as small as possible, crouching against the wall, he led the way into the hotel.

The entrance to the private lift was in the lobby. In a little room behind the reception desk, the receptionist snored softly. Otherwise, it was deserted. Grandma followed Con across the lobby to the lift, but when she saw it she stopped dead.

The lift was the old-fashioned kind, with a folding metal grate that you pulled shut across the entrance.

"That's a cage. I'm not going into a cage, you horrid boy." She was still whispering, but at any moment her whisper would turn into a screech.

"Please, Grandma," whispered Con, "I'll come with you."

Reluctantly, Grandma went in, and Con squeezed in beside her.

Things went better with Ambrose, and Uncle Otto, and Clarence. Ambrose was nervous, but he trusted Con completely. Uncle Otto was brave, and Clarence really enjoyed it, saying "'igher, 'igher" happily until Con shushed him. One by one the yetis were delivered safely to the top floor and introduced to Ellen, shaking hands with her very carefully as they had been taught to do, so as not to break her arm.

At last it was Lucy's turn. But it was horribly difficult to get her into the lift. She really didn't fit. Con pushed and heaved. Finally he got her wedged in sideways, because she was slightly less fat that way than front-to-back, while Con had to crawl in after her and sit on the floor under her stomach. The lift moaned and clanked and squeaked, and Con was sure that they would wake the whole hotel. But they made it to the top, and Ambrose and Clarence

heaved her out with their brute strength. Then they all walked quietly along the corridor, and gathered at the doors of the bridal suite. Con unlocked them and threw them open.

The yetis gasped. There, on the floor in front of them, was an enormous bear-skin rug! It was a very bad moment. The yetis' ear lids turned pale, and Lucy stumbled, almost as if she might faint.

"Bears are our *brothers*, you see," explained Ambrose.

Con and Ellen felt dreadful. After all, how would *they* have felt if they'd been shown into a room and found a child-skin lying on the floor? But when they had apologized and rolled up the rug and put it in a cupboard, the yetis really began to enjoy themselves.

The rooms were splendid; they were very big rooms, which was a good thing, because five yetis take up a lot of space. And all the furniture – the beds, the bath, the sofas and divans – was king-size.

Clarence started turning the electric light on and off, off and on, with a blissful smile on his face. Grandma tried the beds, bouncing up and down, her fur flying. As yetis go, she was a lightweight, only

about twenty-three stone, but it was touch and go whether the beds would survive. Luckily, they were built to take the weight of rajahs and billionaires, who often eat too much and get too little exercise.

Lucy stared in amazement at the dressing-table mirror and said, "Oh, look, everybody! It's me! It's me so clear and beautiful!"

Ambrose, meanwhile, had found the bathroom. "Ooh! What's that? Isn't it *white*! Is it made of snow? Is it for washing your feet in? I can get both feet into it! Ow! Something hot hit me. What's a shower? Uncle Otto, I'm going to have a shower!"

But Otto did not reply. He stood gazing in wonder at a shelf beside the ornate fireplace. "Books," he whispered, "those are books." It is true that the Bible is a wonderful and interesting book, but if you have had nothing else to read for a hundred years or so then even the exciting bits, like Daniel in the Lion's Den or The Witch of Endor, can get a little bit *too* familiar. Now, before his very eyes, were *Flora and Fauna of the Hindu Kush*, *Excitements at the Chalet School*, *How to Win Friends and Influence People*, *The Compleat Angler*, *Nicholas Nickleby*, *The Tatler* (1925-37), *Finn Family Moomintroll* and many, many more. Otto's vast hairy hand wandered lovingly across their spines, and after hesitating for a moment over *The*

Jungle Book settled firmly on *Grimm's Fairy Tales*. Otto sank on to the largest divan and was lost to the world.

Con and Ellen thought they'd never get the yetis to settle for the night – or what was left of it. After Ambrose had had his shower, the bathroom looked like a disaster area and had to be mopped from top to bottom. Then Lucy wanted Ellen to comb the hair on her stomach into a centre parting and make two plaits on either side.

"Like yours," she said.

"But, Lucy, people don't wear plaits on their stomach," said Ellen.

"*People* don't. But yetis might," said Lucy. "It's for Queen Victoria and her children, so they can see out better."

But even when Ellen had made two fat plaits on either side of Lucy's stomach and tied them with the ribbons from her own hair, and they had all found somewhere to sleep – Lucy and Grandma in the two double beds, Ambrose on the sofa, Uncle Otto and Clarence on the Persian carpet – there was still the bedtime story.

"Tell about the Man Bat," begged Ambrose.

"You mean Batman, Ambrose," said Ellen.

Batman and his faithful friend Robin had not

been invented when Lady Agatha came to the valley and the yetis couldn't get enough of him. But even when the children had told them no less than three Batman adventures they weren't through because Clarence started yelling, "'im, 'im," and the others explained that he was saying "hymn" because Lady Agatha had taught the yetis always to end the day with a beautiful song to God. So they all got up again and sang "We Plough the Fields and Scatter", which didn't fit particularly well but was their favourite.

"Do you know what I thought I heard?" said Ambrose drowsily, when he was back on the sofa. "As we came down the mountain?"

"No," said Con. "What?"

"Footsteps," said Ambrose, smiling. He was half asleep. "Following us."

"What sort of footsteps, Ambrose?" asked Ellen.

"Lovely ... ones," murmured Ambrose. "Hoof steps ... and bleating."

Con gazed at him in horror. Not Hubert! It couldn't be! He walked over to the window and drew aside the curtains. In the moonlight, the grass round the hotel was empty, the woods silent and dark.

"There's nothing there," said Con, sighing with relief. And then at last the children tiptoed out, locking the door in case Lucy should walk in her sleep, and went to bed, feeling as tired as they'd ever felt in their lives.

The following morning, Ellen brought the yetis their breakfast and they all said grace. While she explained to Lucy that usually one ate just the cornflakes and not the packet, and told Uncle Otto about marmalade, which was not mentioned in the Bible, and rubbed toothpaste into his bald patch and tied Ambrose's bedsock on again, Con was down in the kitchens explaining things to his father.

Mr Bellamy, the children's father, was a very great chef. His salmon in aspic had been served at the Lord Mayor's Banquet, his peaches in marzipan had been photographed for the cover of a glossy magazine, and society ladies fell over each other, begging him to bake their daughters' wedding cakes.

But like so many great artists, Mr Bellamy was a little

bit *excitable*. When his son (after playing truant the day before) told him that he had hidden five yetis in the Bridal Suite and was going to go with them to England, Mr Bellamy reacted rather strongly. But the egg whisk that he threw whizzed past Con's left ear, the bag of flour exploded in mid-air, and as for the wooden spoon – well, Con had had so many wooden spoons thrown at him in his short life that it might have been a raindrop for all he noticed it. And when he had got his father to agree that the yetis couldn't stay in the Bridal Suite, and that they might as well go to England as anywhere else, he went off to the garage to wait for the lorry.

There were one or two very tough characters who brought the lorries, and no wonder. It was a punishing journey, and towards the end the roads were unspeakable. But when the lorry came at last, a gigantic, articulated vehicle with eighteen wheels, the driver who stepped out, blinking with exhaustion, was one Con had never seen before. A big, burly man with a ginger beard and bright ginger curls – the kind you could have stuck a pencil in and it would have stayed there. But what struck Con most, was what was tattooed on to the man's freckled forearm. Not an anchor or a sailing ship or a heart with "I Love Daisy" in it but ... a *pig*.

Somehow as soon as Con saw that, he knew that he could trust him. A man with a sensible thing like a pig tattooed on his arm *had* to be all right.

"Excuse me," Con said, getting off the pile of tarpaulins on which he'd been sitting, "I know you're tired but could I talk to you? It's important."

"Sure," said the ginger-haired man, whose name was Perry, short for Perrington, which his mother had believed to be a Christian name. "Let's hear it."

"Actually," said Con, "I think you'd better *see* it. Only it's a secret and I mean that." And he led Perry up to the Bridal Suite and knocked in the way that he and Ellen had arranged.

"They're making themselves beautiful for the journey," whispered Ellen, as she opened the door.

They certainly were. Grandma had found some scissors and was cutting her sixteen enormous toenails, bits of which were charging across the room like shrapnel. Lucy had vanished under a pink cloud of talcum powder and, in the bathroom, Uncle Otto, who was a very hygienic yeti, was gargling.

"We had a lovely sleep," said Ambrose, bounding up to Con. "Is this another friend for us? Does he know about that bear called Winnie?"

Perry did not go through the business of pinching himself to see if he was awake. He just wasn't a person who *dreamed* about yetis with blue bedsocks round their necks wanting to know about Winnie the Pooh. Perry's dreams were quite ordinary ones like missing trains or having to play the piano to a huge audience wearing only his underpants.

"All right," he said to Con. "Describe. Explain. Tell."

So Con told him about the secret valley of Nanvi Dar and about Lady Agatha and how he had promised to get the yetis safely to Farley Towers.

"And I want you to take them back in your lorry, instead of whatever you were going to take. It'll be all sealed up: they'll hibernate. No one'll see them."

"Oh, yes? And when I've dropped them off and get back to my bosses with an empty lorry, what then?"

Con fished in his pocket and handed Perry the little bag which Lady Agatha had made out of the hem of her nightgown.

"Wow!" said Perry when he had opened it. "The real stuff. You mean I can give them the price of the goods. The lorry, too, if it comes to that. And there'd still be money over."

"For you," said Con. "A reward for taking us."

"Us?" said Perry. "Are you coming too?"

"I promised I'd deliver them. And I'd like Ellen to come too if I can square it with my father. I really *can't* go making plaits on people's stomachs."

Perry nodded. "There's room in the cab, just about."

He stood looking down into the little flannel bag. Perry had done a lot of things since the day he'd said "Open wide" to a lady called Gladys Girtlestone and

decided he wasn't cut out to be a dentist. He'd been a dishwasher, a road-mender, a lumberjack, and now he was driving lorries.

But not for ever. Perry had a dream and it was a dream to do with pigs.

Perry loved pigs. He loved their fatness and their slowness and their little, suspicious eyes and their disgusting habits. He loved Gloucester Old Spots, which look as though someone has spilt paint on them, and he loved Large Whites, which aren't white but the pink of apple blossom in the spring. He loved Tamworths, which fatten like a dream, and he loved Saddlebacks and Windsors and those black, square, hairy pigs that come from Suffolk.

And what Perry wanted more than anything was to have a pig farm and to breed a completely new pig, the Perrington Porker, which would be a pig to end all pigs, the best pig in the world.

Only, of course, to start a pig farm you need money...

"I'd have taken those crazy animals of yours anyway," said Perry, "because I like them. But if there's a reward I'll have it. Now I'm going to sleep for twenty-four hours. Then I'll go down to Jalpaigun and pick up the load I was supposed to take back. It's mostly dry goods – spices and suchlike, and cloth. I'll drop it at the nunnery – they'll make sure it gets handed out to the poor. Then I'll fix the customs forms and the bumph one needs to get across the borders and change some of the gold into cash for the journey. So ... let's see ... I ought to be ready to leave again by Thursday night. Can you have the yetis in the hotel garage just after midnight? There shouldn't be anyone around then."

Con nodded. "Thanks," he said, holding out his hand. He'd have liked to say more but just then Lucy said, "Sorry!" and began to choke horribly on the talcum powder. You could say a lot about looking after yetis, thought Con, as Ellen climbed on to a chair to thump Lucy on the back, but not that it was *easy*.

It was midnight on the following Thursday. It had taken the yetis a long time to leave the Bridal Suite because they had to say goodbye to everything: "Goodbye, bathroom", "Goodbye, toothpaste", "Goodbye, electric light", and that of course had made them sad and so they'd cried. But now they stood in the hotel garage, staring at the huge, eighteen-wheeled, canary yellow vehicle which was to take them to Britain. On the trailer was an enormous metal container almost as big as a railway carriage. It, too, was painted yellow and on it, in big, black letters, were the words: COLD CARCASSES, INC.

"What's a carcass?" said Grandma suspiciously.

Con and Ellen exchanged glances in the light of the lorry's headlights.

"Well, er, it's sort of ... a cow after it's been ... you know ... ready for eating."

"I thought as much," said Grandma grimly. "Well if anyone thinks I'm travelling halfway round the world labelled a cold carcass – let alone a cold carcass with ink on it – then they can think again."

"Cows are our brothers, you see," explained Ambrose, and the children sighed because they had a feeling that *everybody* was going to be the yetis' brother and though they approved of this and knew it was right, it did seem to make things rather complicated. But fortunately at that point Clarence, who hadn't understood about the carcasses, said, "'ox," which turned out to be "Box" and started climbing into the back of the lorry. After that, the other yetis got in too. There was a big, wide rack for each of them, a bit like a ship's bunk, and a passage down the middle, and a tiny peephole at the end through which they could see into the cab of the lorry and the people in the cab of the lorry could see them. Lucy oozed over the edge of her rack a bit but on the whole they admitted that it was very snug and comfortable.

"When we wake up shall we really be at Farley Towers?" asked Ambrose.

"Really," said Con. "All you have to do is hibernate and leave it to us."

"Only of course we can't hibernate just like *that*," said Ambrose craftily, putting his head on one side and gazing at Ellen. "You'll have to tell us a cold story. The coldest story *ever*."

So while Con turned the freezer to "maximum", Ellen told them about the Snow Queen in her palace of glittering ice, and about little Kay whom she

carried away in her sledge and kept a prisoner, and the yetis thought it was very beautiful and very sad and just about as cold as you could expect a story to be.

And the yetis were just getting very limp and drowsy, and Ellen had just kissed them all goodnight when from the patch of darkness outside the garage door there came a trembly, bleating sound – a sound which turned Con's heart to stone.

"What is it, Con?" asked Ellen.

But there was no need for anybody to tell her. Tottering into the headlights of the lorry, his idiot head waving from side to side, his left horn even more crumpled than it had been in Nanvi Dar, came Hubert.

In a second, Ambrose, his drowsiness forgotten, tumbled from the rack and leaped out of the lorry.

"It's my yak! It's my pet! It's Hubert! It *was* him I heard on the mountain. Oh, Hubert, you'll be able to come to England with us!"

"No!" The words burst from Con. "I can't do it! You've got to tell him to go home."

The other yetis had followed Ambrose out of the lorry. Now they looked rather pityingly at Con. "We *could* say, 'Go home,'" explained Uncle Otto. "We could say, 'Go home' three or four hundred times.

But you may perhaps have noticed that Hubert is not a very *clever* yak."

Con said bitterly that it had crossed his mind. "But we *can't* take him. Ellen, you'll have to get the maids to look after him."

Ellen gave him a worried look. "Con, it's going to take them three days to get the Bridal Suite cleaned up. And you know what a state Dad's in about us going. I just don't think he'll *wear* a yak."

"Oh, please, *please* can't he come? He loves us so much," said Ambrose, and his brown eye started up again.

"Don't you see," said Con. "Yaks don't hibernate. At the other end you'd find him frozen solid. *Dead*."

There was a pause while the yetis took this in and Hubert tried two steps, skidded on a patch of oil and fell flat on his face.

"Couldn't we stay awake? Not be refrigerated?" asked Ambrose.

"Actually, I've a fancy to see a bit of the countryside myself," said Grandma. "Seems a shame to go all that way asleep."

Con bit his lip, thinking hard. Yetis peacefully hibernating were one thing. Yetis awake, needing food, needing exercise, were quite another. There was real danger there.

Hubert gave another plaintive bleat and tottered forward.

"Oh, all right, get the wretched animal in," said Con, making up his mind.

And while Ellen ran back for some powdered milk and a feeding bottle, Con turned off the freezer and slammed the door. Then Perry came from the hotel kitchens carrying a crate of beer and his guitar, and, with a last hug for Mr Bellamy, they got into the cab of the lorry and the long, long journey to Farley Towers began.

6

Aslerfan

The yellow lorry drove on, day after day, down through the foothills of the Himalayas, across the burning plains of India and Pakistan, across Afghanistan with its stony mountains and wild goats and poplar trees, and through the deserts of Iran where the sand got into the yetis' nostrils and between their toes and into their food...

It was not an easy journey. The yetis had to be sealed up inside the lorry until night-time, when they found a deserted place to stop and they could come out and stretch their legs and get some air. The lorry was bumpy and every so often Clarence said "'ick, 'ick," and then Perry would have to quickly try and find a place in which a yeti could be sick without anybody seeing, which was not so easy at all. And, of course, Hubert, who had to be fed from a bottle every four hours, and then turned upside down because he'd swallowed the teat, was just as much of a nuisance as Con had foreseen.

But after a while, the yetis got a taste for travelling. Sitting round the campfire at the end of the day, listening to Perry strum his guitar and pushing Hubert's hooves out of the butter, they felt that this really was life. But when they had said sorry to the last of their condensed milk tins and lay down under the stars to sleep, Con and Ellen always took it in turns to stay awake so that no one should come on the yetis unexpectedly. Nor would they ever let Perry take his turn, however much he grumbled, because they knew that driving a lorry for great distances is the most exhausting thing in the world and that he needed his sleep.

And in this way they travelled very happily until they came to the city of Aslerfan, the capital of the state of Aslerfan, which is wedged like a slice of melon between Iran and Turkey.

Although the yetis couldn't see out, they began to feel queer almost as soon as they crossed the border. Grandma said her corns were shooting and she didn't like the way her liver was carrying on. Lucy kept nervously twisting Queen Victoria and her nine children in her long, blonde fingers; Uncle Otto's face was set and stern.

"I don't *like* this place. It feels funny," said Ambrose the Abominable.

Con and Ellen, sitting in the cab in front, liked it even less. They were approaching the city now.

There were beggars everywhere; the people had grey faces; half-starved mongrel dogs dodged in and out of the traffic. It was dusty and hot and suddenly Ellen drew in her breath because an old man had just crossed the road leading a poor, mangy, limping bear on a chain so tight that he looked as though he must choke.

"It's a dancing bear," Perry explained, while Con made sure that the peephole to the back was tightly shut. "On the way to the palace, I expect. They jab them and put hot coals in their mouth and make them dance for money. Aslerfan's the only place left in the world where you're allowed to do that."

And he explained to the children that Aslerfan was ruled by a cruel and greedy sultan, who lived in luxury in his palace with a fleet of cars and aeroplanes and yachts. The Sultan Midul had five hundred embroidered shirts and twelve hundred pairs of trousers and three fat wives covered from top to toe in diamonds, but his people lived in poverty and squalor. Instead of building schools and hospitals, the Sultan had huge feasts in which everybody gorged themselves till they were sick and began again. Instead of looking after the old and the needy, he organized great hunts in which hundreds of beautiful gazelles and antelopes were cruelly slaughtered. Everybody hated him, but nobody dared to protest because they would just have been put in jail or shot.

"All I ever want to do in Aslerfan," said Perry, "is get through it as quickly as possible."

But Perry reckoned without the lorry.

Perry's lorry looked all right from the outside, but its inside was more like that of an ailing old lady than a twenty-tonne truck. Its carburettor got choked up as soon as you breathed on it, its exhaust pipe hung on by willpower and string and the engine sounded like an old hen with the croup. And now, just when they wanted to get through Aslerfan quickly, the wretched lorry began to boil.

"Oh, Lord!" said Perry. "Not the water pump."

But it was. "We'll have to spend the night here, I'm afraid, while I get this thing fixed," said Perry worriedly. "I'll find as quiet a place to park as I can but for goodness' sake don't let the yetis out. You saw that bear..."

So he parked in a quiet street not far from the Sultan's palace. Beside it was a little park, with a few dusty date palms, a tobacco kiosk and a public lavatory. And at the far side, something else. A zoo.

The yetis had never before had to spend a night in a town, let alone a town like Aslerfan. It meant that they couldn't get out and say, "Sorry, grass," and build a campfire and stretch their legs, but had to stay cooped up in the lorry, which was stiflingly hot because Perry had disabled the refrigeration system to get at the water pump. But the yetis understood that it was necessary and they were very good.

While Perry went to find a garage and Con went shopping for some fruit, Ellen slipped into the little park to buy some lemonade for the yetis from a kiosk. When she came back, she was very quiet and pale.

"Are you sad?" said Ambrose, and his brown eye got ready in case there was any crying to be done.

But Ellen just shook her head and said it was nothing, or perhaps the heat. And then Con returned and they had a picnic in the back and they were just getting ready for the bedtime story when the noises began.

They were bad noises: howls of misery; roars of loneliness; whimpers of pain.

Even by the light of his torch, Con could see the yetis' ear lids turn pale and Lucy, who had just taken her seventh banana, put it down untouched.

"That was a poor lion who's got no meat to say 'sorry' to," she said, as an ear-splitting roar filled the night.

"That elephant has got a pain in his trunk," said Uncle Otto worriedly.

"And listen to those poor seals coughing their lungs out," said Grandma.

Con was amazed. "How do you know which animals are which and what they're saying?" he asked. "You've never seen lions or seals or elephants, have you?"

Ambrose turned his wall eyes reproachfully on Con. "But they're our *brothers*," he said.

Con sighed. He'd asked for that one. "Look, it's just a zoo. All animals make noises at night in a zoo—"

But Ellen, usually so quiet and gentle, interrupted him. "No, Con, it's an awful place, this. I saw it when I was getting the lemonade. The cages are filthy and far too small; there are flies everywhere; the monkeys are full of sores and the antelopes have got foot rot... And there's a ghastly sort of dungeon place where they throw the dancing bears that are too old to work."

It was true. The Aslerfan Zoo was a disgrace. But it was the Sultan's private zoo and when people in the city complained, he just laughed. As for the head keeper, a man called Mr Bullaby, he took the money he was paid for the animals and used it for himself. So the animals were sick and cramped and underfed, and hundreds died every year from loneliness or bad feeding or disease.

Con bit his lip, frowning. Cruelty to animals always made him feel completely sick and hollow. But he'd given his word that he'd get the yetis to Farley Towers and that meant keeping them cheerful and keeping them safe. So he began to tell them "Rumpelstiltskin", making up such funny names for the Queen to guess that Ambrose nearly fell off his bunk laughing, and after they had *whispered*, "Lead, Kindly Light" (because there were still strollers about in the streets who might have thought it odd if a load of Cold Carcasses had started singing hymns) the children slipped to the front and curled up in the cab and fell asleep.

But the yetis couldn't sleep. Even when they shut their ear lids they could still *feel* the noises from that dreadful zoo.

And presently Ambrose leaned down from his bunk and said "Grandma?"

"What is it?" said Grandma, opening her ear lids.

"I was thinking ... Ellen was sad about that zoo, wasn't she?"

Grandma nodded. "And no wonder."

"Con was sad too," said Lucy. "He didn't say anything but his face was all screwed up and tight."

"So we could give them a surprise," said Ambrose. "Con and Ellen, I mean. Because they've been so good to us."

"'urprise," said Clarence happily, nodding.

"What sort of a surprise, Ambrose?" asked Lucy.

"A lovely one," said Ambrose, his blue eye beaming. "We could let all the animals out of their cages. Now, while it's dark. And in the morning they'd all be happy and free."

There was a pause while the yetis considered this.

"Do As You Would Be Done By," said Grandma presently, "that's what Lady Agatha said. Only God said it first. How would we like to be shut up in filthy cages?"

And then they all turned their enormous heads towards Uncle Otto, who was really the head of the family now that Father was no longer with them.

Uncle Otto hesitated. He understood perhaps better than the others how important it was for the yetis to keep out of people's way. But just then there came a sound more terrible than any they had heard yet: the wings of the thirst-maddened birds of prey beating against the wire of their appalling cages.

Uncle Otto made up his mind. And a few moments later, leaving Hubert tied to one of the bunks, the yetis had pushed aside the iron bar which closed the back of the lorry and were climbing over the high barbed wire which surrounded the zoo.

As soon as they dropped down inside the enclosure, the noises stopped. It was as though the animals knew that their time of torture was over. The lions stopped their restless pacing and stood silent and golden-eyed, waiting. The giraffes hung their poor, stiff necks over the bars of their pen and blew softly and hopefully through their velvet lips. The weary old bears got up on their hind legs and danced of their own free will.

"Right," said Uncle Otto. He had left his woolly

hat in the lorry and in the moonlight his bald patch shone like the shield of St George. "Let us begin."

The next two hours were the busiest of the yetis' lives. When Lady Agatha had warned Con about the yetis' strength, she hadn't been exaggerating. They bent iron bars like plasticine, broke locks with a couple of fingers, uprooted railings as if they were dandelions...

Uncle Otto freed the big cats: the lions and tigers and panthers and jaguars, and they rubbed themselves, soft as kittens,

82

against his legs before loping off joyfully into the night. Clarence helped out the poor, rheumaticky old hippopotamuses and rhinoceroses, who had almost forgotten how to walk, and led the elephants, with their sore trunks and runny eyes, into a clump of palm trees where they could feed. Lucy let out the little things that had huddled sadly on the concrete floors of their smelly runs for years: opossums like old handbags, scruffy little moonrats and dik-diks and bushbabies, which she shook out and sat gently on their feet before they scampered gratefully away.

Grandma, meanwhile, had got hold of a hose and was washing down the sea lions and walruses and alligators, who were covered in green slime from their disgusting, sludgy ponds. "Now off you go, and get down to the river quickly," she scolded a crocodile who was lying on his back, letting the hose play over his stomach and showing his poor, broken teeth in the first real smile he'd smiled since the cruel Sultan's men had caught him in their nets. And it was marvellous to see how every animal, even the most stupid like the anteaters, or the fiercest like the cougars, or the shyest like the gazelles, found time to thank the yetis with a grateful nibble, a friendly lick or a thankful hiss, before they crawled or slithered or hopped off to freedom.

The dancing bears were the last to go. It was as if they could hardly tear themselves away from the yetis and even when they had shuffled off into the darkness they came back again and again to rub themselves once more against their rescuers.

But at last the zoo was empty and the yetis were just turning to go back to the lorry when Lucy said:

"Where's Ambrose? And what's that splash?"

What that splash was, was Mr Bullaby, the head keeper, whom Ambrose the Abominable had just thrown into the crocodile pond.

"I found him in his house, hiding under the bed," said Ambrose, when the others ran up to him, "and I thought he ought to be punished. Lady Agatha always punished us when we were naughty and this zoo is *more* than naughty, isn't it?"

The yetis stood round solemnly in the moonlight, watching Mr Bullaby in his yellow silk pyjamas, floundering and spluttering in the filthy pool.

"Was I wrong to do it?" asked Ambrose, suddenly growing anxious.

But the others, remembering the pitiful things they had seen that night, said no, he hadn't been.

"If the crocodiles had still been there, you shouldn't have done it," said Lucy, "because it wouldn't have been fair on the crocodiles. But they weren't. So you should've."

And then they all padded quietly out of the zoo and climbed back into the lorry and fell asleep.

Con, curled up in the cab in front, was having a most peculiar dream. He dreamed that a large and rather loopy-looking gnu was looking in at the lorry window.

Making an effort, he opened his eyes, stretched...

A large and loopy-looking gnu *was* looking in at the lorry window.

"Goodness!" said Con. But before he could explore further, Perry came back from the all-night garage carrying the mended pump. "The place's gone mad," he said. "There's a tree sloth hanging from the lamp post, a couple of kangaroos are window shopping in the square and—" He broke off. "Good Lord! Look at the zoo!"

In silence, Perry and the children stared across the little park at the broken fences, the shattered buildings...

"Is it an earthquake, do you think?" asked Ellen, who'd only just woken up and was still rather muddled.

"Or a terrorist letting off bombs?" suggested Con.

But before they could decide how the zoo had got into the state it was in, there was an agitated scrabbling from the container and when Con cautiously opened the door, all five yetis stood looking out at him, beaming with pride and joy.

"We did it! It's a surprise for you! We let out all the animals, every single one!" said Ambrose the Abominable.

There was a moment of total silence while Con

took this in. "Oh no! You didn't! Say you didn't!" he begged.

"But we did. All the animals were *sad* so—"

Con's face had turned ashen. He had begun to tremble. "Don't you see, it's a *crime*. Breaking up people's property, smashing things... As soon as the Sultan gets to hear of it, he'll send his soldiers with machine guns. You'll be mown down, you'll be—"

But Perry now came to the rescue. "We're only a hundred miles from the border," he said, "and the Sultan can't touch us once we're across. The pump's mended; no one's about yet – we've a good chance of making a getaway."

And a few seconds later the door had shut on the bewildered yetis and the yellow lorry was roaring out of the city.

A hundred miles in a slow and overloaded lorry can seem like a desperately long way. Every motor horn, every train whistle made the children jump as they imagined the Sultan's men come to round up the yetis or torture them or simply shoot them out of hand.

But the Sultan did not come that day, or any other day. And that was because, by evening, the city of Aslerfan no longer had a sultan.

What happened was this. On the morning that the yellow lorry left Aslerfan, the cruel and greedy little Sultan woke up in his huge gold and turquoise bed as he did each day, stretched his fat little arms as he did each day, and thought of all the nice things he was going to do, like watching a public execution, having some journalists flogged because they'd dared to criticize him in their newspapers and arranging a hunt in which a herd of exquisite fallow deer would be gunned down from his private fleet of helicopters.

Then, as he did every day, he rang for his servants. But after that, things happened differently. Because what came into the room was not his barber to shave him, or his valet to dress him, or his footman carrying the six fried eggs he always ate for breakfast.

It was a hippopotamus.

"Help! screamed the Sultan. "Help! Help!" He reached for the bell rope and pulled it again. Only it was not the bell rope, it was the tail of an enormous boa constrictor, which now fell in a hissing and annoyed heap on to the Sultan's embroidered counterpane.

"Aaeee!" yelled the Sultan. He leaped out of bed and rushed for the nearest door, which led into his lapis lazuli and marble bathroom.

Sitting quietly in the middle of the bath was a huge, whiskery and very wrinkled walrus.

"It's a plague! It's a plague of animals! The gods have decided to punish me!" yelled the Sultan, who had read about the great plagues of Egypt, when Jehovah had sent locusts and frogs and flies to punish a wicked ruler who had been cruel to his people.

As the terrified Sultan ran through the corridors of his palace, he saw more and more signs that the gods were out to get him. An orang-utan was crouching on the imperial throne, dreamily cracking fleas between his teeth; a proud ostrich had just laid

an egg on the grand piano in the music room, and three armadillos were bulldozing their way across the table in the state dining hall...

Still in his pyjamas, the fat little man reached the main courtyard. There was no sign of his servants or his soldiers, who had all fled when the animals invaded the palace. But standing by the fountain, looking at him through golden, serious eyes, were two very stripy tigers.

The Sultan waited no longer. With a scream of terror he turned and ran, on and on, through his terraced gardens, and private parks and pleasure pavilions, on and on, till he came to the brown bare hills that surrounded the city. And there he fell on his knees and beat his head against the earth and asked the gods to forgive him his sins. And the next day he put on a sacking robe and went to live in a cave where he spent the rest of his life gabbling prayers and fasting so that he would get to heaven in the end.

And so the hated Sultan was seen no more, and in the city of Aslerfan there was feasting and rejoicing and dancing in the streets. People hugged each other and let off fireworks and threw open the doors of their cafés so that everyone could eat and drink their fill. The prisoners were let out of their dungeons and the sick were taken off the streets and cared for. But because it was the animals who had brought freedom to the people, the new government made it a law that all the animals that had escaped were to be guests of the city and not to be harmed. So, for many months, while they built a new, model zoo for those animals that preferred to live in town, you could see giraffes dozing in the middle of the road while cars edged carefully around them, barbers politely shaving wildebeests who had wandered into their shops, or old ladies giving lifts to porcupines in their shopping baskets.

Nor did anyone ever find out who had freed the animals. True, Mr Bullaby had gabbled something about furry giants with bedsocks round their necks and Queen Victoria on their stomachs. But when people talk like that there is only one thing to do: take them to some nice, quiet hospital and shut them up till they are better. And that is exactly what the people of Aslerfan did.

7

The St Bernards of Feldenberg

The yellow lorry had passed through the beautiful city of Istanbul and was well into Turkey before Con stopped shivering and peering into the driving mirror to see if anyone was following them. Only when Perry went into a café in a little dusty village where they had stopped for petrol, and heard on the wireless that the Sultan of Aslerfan had fled, did the children relax.

Unfortunately, the news that they had saved the people of Aslerfan from their cruel Sultan made the yetis very smug.

"We did *good*, didn't we?" said Ambrose, his blue eye beaming. "We're sort of *rescuing* yetis now."

"Well, don't be rescuing yetis again, please," said Con, who'd really had a dreadful fright. "Not till you're safe at Farley Towers."

That night Perry found a beautiful deserted little bay on the Sea of Marmara with a track down which the lorry could just go. Lucy and Grandma paddled, lifting the long hair on their legs out of the water like Lady Agatha had shown them, and Ambrose tethered Hubert to a fig tree and told him that he was a big yak now and could eat grass perfectly well if he tried. Con made a bonfire and they sat round it while Perry told them just how he thought the Perrington Porker would look when he had bred it: pink and fat but very strong, with a double-jointed tail and droopy ears, because pigs with droopy ears are more peace-loving than the other kind.

"Can we play the Farley Towers game?" begged Ambrose, as they lay down under the stars to sleep. It was a game that Ellen had invented to while away the journey and the yetis loved it.

"What will we do on our first day at Farley Towers?" said Lucy, because that was the way the game began.

"On the first day you'll have dinner by candlelight with damask napkins," said Ellen.

"What will we do on the second day?" said Ambrose.

"On the second day you'll have tea on the lawn with strawberries and cream in crystal bowls," said Ellen.

"'ird?" said Clarence. "'ird?"

But they never discovered what they would do on their third day at Farley Towers because at that moment Hubert decided he had seen his mother.

Hubert had been seeing his mother ever since

they'd left Nanvi Dar. In fact, when he wasn't swallowing his teat or trying to dig Hubert Holes inside the lorry, seeing his mother was what Hubert did. But up to now his mother, though unlikely, had been *possible*: a stray goat, a distant, browsing sheep, that sort of thing. Whereas what Hubert was now straining to reach, bleating with delight, seemed to be a rusty heap of scrap metal which somebody had left on the beach.

Sighing, the yetis got up again to look.

"No, dear," said Grandma sternly, "that's not your mother. That's a wheelbarrow."

And shaking their enormous heads, the yetis returned to their beds and fell asleep.

They travelled steadily north, through Greece with its ruined temples and its olive groves; through the long, flat plain of the Western Balkans with its storks and fields of maize, until they came to the little country of Feldenberg, in the foothills of the Alps.

And now there were pine forests and clear, rushing rivers and the sound of cowbells from the meadows. The air grew cool, the trim, wooden houses had boulders on the roof to weigh them down against the wind, and in the distance, white as icing sugar, were the glaciers of the Alpine peaks.

"Oh, isn't it beautiful, it's just like home!" cried the yetis when they were allowed to get out for a moment and have a stretch.

"Can I have some leather pants like that?" begged Ambrose, who had glimpsed, in a distant field, a little boy in lederhosen.

But Grandma had noticed something even more exciting. "What's that noise?" she said eagerly, and Con explained that it was yodelling, a sort of cross between calling each other and singing, which people did on mountains.

"I can do that!" said Grandma. "I just know I can." She threw back her head. "Yodel-aaa-eee-ooo," yodelled Grandma. "Yodel-aaa-eee-ooo!"

"Oh, hush, Grandma," begged the children, while all around there was the sound of ear lids thudding shut, "suppose someone hears you?"

But it was no use. Yodelling is like a drug once it gets hold of you and it had certainly got hold of Grandma. And it was with Grandma still going strong that they drove up towards the High Alps, and the pass which ran between the towering crags of the Death Peak to the east and the zigzag range of the Emperor Mountains to the west.

"It's going to be quite a pull with this load on," said Perry. "Cold at the top, too. I think we'll stop off for a proper meal."

So he parked the lorry by a deserted mill on the edge of a pretty village with an onion-domed church, a cobbled square and an inn with carved wooden shutters and a white horse painted on a sign above the door. And when he explained to the yetis that the children ought to have something hot before the next part of the journey, they all promised to be as quiet as mice and keep the peephole tightly shut.

The inn had red-checked tablecloths, wooden benches and nice, old-fashioned paintings on the walls showing brave St Bernard dogs with barrels round their necks saving people from the snow. And while Con and Ellen waded through their huge helpings of liver soup with dumplings, and pickled cabbage with ham, and nut cake with whipped cream, Perry, who spoke a little German, got talking to the innkeeper and his guests.

And what they were all talking about – very angrily – was a mad Englishman called Harry Letts.

Mr Letts was a very rich and very important television tycoon who had come to spend his holiday in the village with his little son, a boy of nine, called Leo. Everybody liked Leo, who was a friendly, quiet, rather dreamy child, but nobody liked Mr Letts, who had gone round telling anyone who would listen that his son was a spoilt, namby-pamby boy ruined by his mother and that he, Harold Letts, was going to make a man of him or else.

So that very morning he had set out with the little boy to climb the Death Peak. And the Death Peak, which towered above the village, was the highest, most dangerous mountain in Feldenberg.

"He is a criminal, a lunatic," said the innkeeper

angrily, wiping his counter clean. "Even an experienced person would not risk the Peak today, with a storm coming up."

"A storm?" said the children, surprised, when Perry told them what had been said. The sun shone; the icing sugar peaks stood out against a pale blue sky.

But the yetis, when they got back to them, nodded their huge heads wisely. "Oh, yes, a storm's coming. A bad one," they said. "We can always tell because the hair on the back of our knees goes tingly."

And sure enough, as the lorry ground its way slowly up the winding road, gradually leaving behind the lush meadows and fruit-hung orchards, the sun vanished behind clouds, the peaks turned mouse-coloured and sinister, the wind freshened...

"Poor Leo," thought Con, looking up at the crags of the Death Peak where the rain that was now lashing their windscreen would, he knew, be falling as drifting, blinding snow. And he thought with a pang of homesickness of his own father, who might sometimes throw bags of flour, but who never came up with idiot ideas like making a man of his son.

About three hundred feet below the top of the pass, Perry gave up. The lorry had started its chicken-with-the-croup noises, and though the windscreen wipers were working at the double it was impossible to keep the windows clear of sleet. To try and make the descent down one of the most dangerous and winding roads in Europe in weather like that would have been madness, even with an empty lorry. As it was...

So he turned off into a deserted quarry, which ran off the curve of the road and provided some shelter. "We'll have to spend the night here, I'm afraid," he said.

The yetis, of course, loved the idea. "Isn't it *fresh*, isn't it bracing?" they said, and for an awful moment it looked as though Grandma would begin to yodel again.

But after a while, Con and Perry began to get worried about Ellen. It was bitterly cold at that height, and though they kept the windows tightly closed, the chill seeped right through their clothes and the thin army blanket which was all they had for covering. Ellen never complained, but she was a frail, slight child and now she had no way of hiding the whiteness of her face or the shivering fits which shook her.

"Listen," said Perry to Con, "do you see that building up there, on the Death Peak? On that rocky ledge?"

Con nodded.

"It's a monastery. The monks that run it are great people – they're always helping travellers in trouble. They train St Bernards too – those mountain rescue dogs. You can reach it in half an hour and the path's perfectly safe."

"You mean I should take Ellen up there and ask if we can spend the night?"

"That's right. But go now, quickly. You've only another hour till dark."

"But what about the yetis?" said Con.

"I'll look after them. They'll be all right, I promise."

Con threw another glance at Ellen, huddled in the corner of the cab and trying to stop her teeth from chattering. "All right," he said.

An hour later, safe from the storm, the children were sitting over steaming bowls of soup and hunks of fresh-baked bread in the monastery dining hall.

It was a beautiful room. Candles burnt on the long wooden table; there were heavy, carved oak settles and a blazing fire of pine logs in which the resin bubbled and sang.

But what Con and Ellen couldn't take their eyes off, was what was lying in a huge, warm huddle of feet and melting eyes and thumping tails across the hearth. Five dogs. Five of the most beautiful dogs they had ever seen: white and brown; gold and liver-coloured; fawn and mahogany, with wrinkled foreheads and slobbery jowls. The famous St Bernards of Feldenberg.

And while the children ate their soup, the friendly monks, clustering round, told them – in a jumble of languages – the story of the dogs.

For a long time, they explained, people had stopped using dogs for mountain rescue work because they were so expensive to train and modern devices like helicopters and radar seemed to make them unnecessary. But a very rich and kind American, an oil millionaire from Texas, who had come to Feldenberg for a holiday, had been so upset to think that those wonderful dogs were no longer bred and

trained, that he had sent the monks a litter of five of the most highly bred St Bernards in America – *and* given the monastery a huge sum of money to be used each year for the feeding and training of the dogs.

"How marvellous!" said Con, scratching the ear of an enormous white-and-liver-coloured brute who had fallen asleep across his feet. "And have they rescued anyone yet?"

The monks looked at each other and said, no. Fortunately, the Death Peak was a very dangerous mountain which people treated with respect, so nobody had *needed* rescuing. A silence fell. And then, suddenly, perhaps because Con and Ellen had very *listening* faces, it all came out.

The dogs, said Brother Peter (and all the others nodded to show that they agreed with him) were the most charming, gentle animals that anyone could wish for. The monks adored them; they couldn't bear to think of life without them. There was only one snag. They were absolutely useless at rescuing anyone from anything.

The children found this almost impossible to believe.

"But I thought ... *all* St Bernards..." stammered Con.

The monks shook their heads and sighed. Most, perhaps, but not all. Certainly not Baker or Brutus or Biscuit and quite definitely not Bouncer or Beelzebub.

And one by one, kind Brother Peter, who was in charge of the kennels, introduced the dogs and explained their little troubles.

Baker, it seemed, suffered from chilblains – nasty big pink lumps which came up as soon as he set foot in the snow. Brutus, on the other hand, couldn't stand heights. They had lifted Brutus on to a table once to have his toenails cut and he had very nearly fainted. Biscuit was terrified of the dark and had to have a night light in his kennel. Bouncer, a real bruiser of a dog whose muscles beneath his brindled fur rippled like steel, cried like a baby when he had to wet his feet.

"But that one?" said Ellen. "That huge dark one over there?"

The monks blushed. What was wrong with Beelzebub seemed to be a little different. Then, very shyly, Brother Peter leaned forward and whispered: "He drinks."

And he explained that every St Bernard was sent off with a keg of brandy round his neck so that when the lost traveller was found he could have a healing sip. Beelzebub, however, was driven so mad by the smell of brandy that he simply shattered the keg against the first rock he could find, lapped up the contents – and had to be carried home and put to bed.

And because the monks were good and honest men they had decided that it wasn't fair to go on deceiving the people of Feldenberg and taking the American's money, so they had decided to send the dogs away the very next day. "But it will be like giving away our children," said Brother Peter, and all the monks looked so sad, that for a moment, Con and Ellen, used as they were to yetis, expected them all to burst into tears.

"But if no one ever *needs* rescuing," said Ellen, who couldn't bear anyone to be unhappy, "what does it matter?"

What happened next was just like a play or a film. There was a violent pounding on the door and a man stumbled forward into the room. He was dressed in climbing clothes, his face was badly cut and bruised and his leg dragged as he came forward.

"Help! I must have help quickly! It's my son, my little Leo. He's lost on the Death Peak. Send out the dogs to save him! Please ... quickly ... send out ... the dogs," said Mr Letts – and Brother Peter was just in time to catch him as he fell.

8

On Death Peak

The monks put out the dogs. What else could they do? They pushed out Biscuit, howling because of the terrifying darkness, and Baker, trying to keep his chilblained feet out of the snow. They pushed out Brutus, who got giddy on a kitchen table, and the whimpering Bouncer and boozy Beelzebub with his barrel...

And then, while the younger monks went down to the village for help, the rest of them went back into the dining hall and waited for disgrace and ruin.

Con had known all along, really, what he had to do. When a child's life was at stake you had to take a chance. Even Lady Agatha, he knew, would have wanted him to let the yetis out. Only they could save Leo.

He went over to the fire where Ellen was helping to care for the delirious Mr Letts as he rambled and blamed himself for the accident. Then he slipped out of the monastery and, with his head bent against the gale, ran back downhill towards the yellow lorry.

The yetis when he reached them understood at once. "Don't worry, my boy," said Uncle Otto reassuringly, "we shall find him. Remember, we can see in the dark."

"After all, we are *rescuing* yetis," said Ambrose smugly – and while Perry made his way down to the village to join a stretcher party, and Con set off for the monastery once more, the yetis padded up the steep sides of the quarry and were gone.

Even for the yetis it was bitterly cold on the Death Peak. As they padded across the treacherous glacier, leaped crevasses, peered into gulleys, the snow beat against their faces and the wind scythed like a rapier through their fur. But they let nothing hinder them in their search for Leo. Patiently, clinging with their eight toes on to knife edges of ice, they squeezed down chimneys of rock, dug into snowdrifts, raked the darkness with their saucer eyes...

There was nothing. No answer to their calls. No trace of the boy.

"I don't want him to be dead," said Ambrose in a quavery voice, clambering up a pinnacle of ice. "I don't want anyone to be dead, *ever*."

But things were beginning to look very bad for Leo. And now Grandma was in trouble. She was, after all, over four hundred years old. Shivering fits shook her, her breath came in painful gasps, her legs felt like matchsticks.

"Come on, you stupid old yeti," she scolded herself. "Here's a poor child in trouble and you totter about like an old blancmange."

But though she was cross with herself, she couldn't make her heart pump harder or her muscles pull her up the towering cliffs of rock.

"I'll just rest for a moment," said Grandma. "I'll crawl into this little cave here and then I'll be as right as rain."

She dragged herself into the cave and flopped down on a slab of stone, but still she couldn't seem to catch her breath. Grandma did not often feel old and sad and useless, but she felt it now.

And then, in the back of the cave, she saw

something stir: a fair blur; a faint, small shape. She moved closer, bent over it.

And after that she didn't feel old and sad and useless any more; she felt as happy as she'd ever felt in her life. She had found Leo.

And now a solemn procession wound itself down the Death Peak towards the monastery below.

First came Uncle Otto; path-finding, responsible and serious. Then came Ambrose, beaming with pride because Grandma, who was still feeling rather tottery, had let him carry Leo. Tottery she might be, but not so tottery that she couldn't constantly peer over Ambrose's shoulder and tell him what to do with the boy.

"Gently, now, don't let his neck hang like that, support his head, that's right. Mind that leg..."

Behind Grandma came Lucy, her gentle blue eyes full of pity for Leo, who lay, still as a leaf, with closed eyes in Ambrose's arms.

They were just starting to cross the glacier when Clarence, who was bringing up the rear, suddenly stopped.

"'og," said Clarence firmly.

The others sighed. It was so important to bring the boy to safety quickly.

"No, Clarence, there's no bog here, the ground's as hard as nails," said Lucy soothingly.

"And there certainly aren't any *logs*," said Grandma. "We're much too high for trees."

But Clarence kept on pointing and suddenly they saw what he meant. Wedged between two boulders, lying flat on his back with his chilblained feet stuck in the air like table legs, was a large and frost-covered St Bernard.

They had found Baker.

It was an embarrassing moment for the yetis. They knew that St Bernards were famous for rescuing people and it did not seem right just to pick the dog up as if he were a baby. But Baker, frenziedly wagging his tail, made it clear that he expected just that, and it was with a St Bernard hanging like a gigantic, snuffling muffler round Clarence's neck that the party moved on.

They didn't so much *find* Biscuit as fall over him. He was rolled into a whimpering ball of fur, half-covered in snow, and even when Lucy picked him up and hung him over her shoulders he refused to open his eyes. No one was going to get Biscuit to look into that awful darkness.

Brutus and Bouncer were lying together under an outcrop of rock. Brutus must have got giddy and fallen from it because he had passed out cold. Bouncer was trying to dry his feet in Brutus's armpits.

"This is a very strange mountain," said Uncle Otto, picking up the dogs and tucking one under each arm. "It seems to erupt dogs."

But the mountain had not finished with them yet.

As they came off the glacier on to the last stretch of scree before the monastery, they heard a most unexpected sound.

Somewhere, close by, someone was hiccuping.

Like an old warhorse scenting battle, Grandma lifted her grizzled head. "Wait here for me," she said grimly.

She stumped off down a little gulley. When she came back she was half dragging, half carrying, the large, befuddled and sheepish-looking Beelzebub.

"You disgusting brute," she was yelling at him, "Don't you know what drink does to your liver? Do you want to end up in the gutter?" And all the way down the mountain, Grandma, her grey hand clamped like iron round Beelzebub's collar, threatened him with an Early Grave, an Alcoholic Dogs' Home and a Beating He'd Never Forget.

But now they had arrived at the monastery gates. Very gently, Ambrose lowered Leo on to the ground beneath a clump of wind-gnarled firs. Then the others put down the dogs. This was hard to do because the dogs most definitely did not want to be put down, but the yetis were firm.

There was only one more thing to do and Grandma did it. Filling her scrawny chest with air, she threw back her head and yodelled.

And then, carefully leaping from rock to rock so as not to leave footprints on the snowy ground, the yetis vanished.

And so when Con, with the monks at his heels, came rushing out, they found the five dogs clustered in a warm and sheltering huddle round the little boy – and no one else in sight.

"He's safe! The dogs have rescued him!" cried Con, crossing his fingers inside the pocket of his anorak. "They must have done!"

"No … it can't be," stammered Brother Peter. "It would have to be a miracle."

But the monks were men of God. They were *used* to miracles. If God could make five loaves and two fishes go round five thousand people – well, maybe he could make some of the silliest dogs in the world carry out the most heroic mountain rescue of the century. And as they carried the little boy gently in to the warmth of the fire and put him down beside his joyful father, it was all the monks could do to stop dancing and singing and shouting, they were so happy.

So far from being sent away, Baker and Brutus and Biscuit, Bouncer and Beelzebub became the most famous dogs in the land. Stories were written about them in the papers; they appeared on television; statues of them were put up in the village square. The American who bred them sent the monks even more money so that they were able to build a new chapel with the most beautiful bells that pealed across the valley, and everyone who passed through Feldenberg stopped off and climbed the steep path to the monastery to gaze at the lion-hearted dogs. But after the accident to the Englishman and his little boy, no one was allowed to go climbing on the Death Peak without a proper guide, so there were no more disasters. Which was just as well, because for the rest of their long and happy lives, Baker had chilblains, Brutus got giddy, Biscuit had to have a night light in his kennel and Bouncer refused to wet his feet. Only Beelzebub got a bit better. Sometimes he would take a little Coca-Cola with his brandy. But only sometimes...

As for Leo, there were no bones broken; he only needed quiet and warmth. But the first night in the hospital in Feldenberg he was restless and stirred in his sleep and said: "My ... furry animals ... I want ... my furry things." And the night sister, who knew children who are ill often act younger than their years, went and fetched him a teddy bear from the cupboard in the children's ward. But fortunately by that time Leo was fast asleep.

9

El Magnifico

For two days after they had rescued Leo from the mountain, the yetis stayed quietly hidden in a thick fir wood on the borders of Feldenberg and Switzerland.

The reason for this was Grandma's tonsils. After her last great yodel outside the gates of the monastery, Grandma's tonsils had snapped. At least she *said* they had snapped and Grandma wasn't the sort of person you argued with. Certainly her voice was very croaky; yodelling was out of the question and she seemed frail and tired. So Perry took the lorry down a long, deserted track leading into the forest and parked it by a disused timber mill and they shut up the lorry and took to the woods.

It was beautiful amongst the firs. The grass was soft and mossy; there were red and white toadstools, and bilberries which tasted delicious and made their teeth a rich, dark blue. There was a stream to paddle in and fir cones for Clarence to play with and squirrels to be Ambrose's friends. Grandma rested and Ellen had a Great Combing of all the yetis so that their fur shone again and their silky hair blew in

the wind. She polished Queen Victoria and washed Ambrose's bedsock and she rubbed Uncle Otto's bald patch with resin from the pine trees so that it became the most sweetly scented bald patch in the world. Perry stopped worrying about the insides of the wretched lorry and just lay under the trees smoking his pipe and thinking of his Porker. Even Con forgot to be anxious and when he climbed trees it was more for fun than to see if anyone was coming.

It is always when you are having a lovely and carefree time that the most unfortunate things happen. On the afternoon of their second day in the woods, they were sitting peacefully by the banks of the stream. Clarence was pretending to catch fish; Perry was strumming his guitar. Even Hubert had sensibly decided that a sawn-off tree stump was not, after all, his mother and was making quite a good job of cropping the grass.

"What will we do on the *sixth* day?" said Ambrose, rubbing his head against Ellen's arm.

"On the sixth day you will waltz in the great ballroom beneath crystal chandeliers," said poor Ellen, who sometimes wished she'd never invented the Farley Towers game.

"What will we do on the seventh—"

"AAAAEEEE!"

The terrified scream rang through the forest, sending Hubert head first into a blackberry bush, scattering the birds...

They all scrambled to their feet. Staring at them from the other side of the brook was a fat, apple-cheeked girl in a dirndl, carrying a basket of bilberries. Two flaxen plaits stuck out from her head, her mouth was open and her pale blue eyes were wide with terror.

"*Mutter! Mutter! Mutter!*" yelled the girl and, dropping her basket, she turned and fled screeching through the forest.

"I don't call that a mutter," said Ambrose, who was rather hurt at the way she was carrying on. "I call that a scream."

But Perry, his face serious, said *Mutter* was the German for mother. The girl was looking for her parents. And when she had found them...

"Back to the lorry at once, at once!" said Con, all his old worries flooding back. "Oh, quickly, *quickly*."

And gathering Hubert up as they fled, the yetis followed him.

Even Perry was disturbed by what had happened. "If the kid saw the lorry and connected it with the yetis ... and if her parents believe her and don't just think the yetis were wild bears... It could be awkward."

"Awkward! It could be a disaster," said Con, sitting pale as death beside Perry and blaming himself again and again for not having kept a better lookout in the woods.

"They could make me open up the lorry," Perry went on. "And even if they don't harm the yetis there's all that business about quarantine. No animal's supposed to come into the country without at least six months in quarantine. If they *are* animals. On the other hand, if they're people they're illegal immigrants, so at best they'd be sent straight back."

"Isn't there *anything* we can do?" said Con frantically.

"Well..." said Perry, his forehead furrowed up. "If they spotted that the lorry is British they'll be expecting us to go north, straight through Germany or France and on to one of the Channel ports. Suppose we turn west instead, and go out through Spain? There's a new ferry boat service from San Vigo which takes heavy lorries. It's a heck of a long way round, but I reckon we'd have a better chance of getting through without any questions being asked."

So the yellow lorry turned westwards towards Spain. Spain is a beautiful country with famous castles, carved balconies, vineyards and chestnut groves.

But there was one thing about Spain that they had forgotten...

*

They reached the little town of Santa Maria in the late afternoon. Flags were flying, a band was playing in the park and the streets were packed with gaily dressed people buying doughnuts and nougat and fizzy lemonade from market stalls.

"Oh, heck," said Perry, "we've hit a bullfight day. It's going to take us ages to get through this traffic."

"A bullfight?" said Grandma, when Con repeated this to the yetis in the back. "But bulls shouldn't be *allowed* to fight. Why doesn't someone throw a bucket of cold water over them?"

Con bit his lip. "It isn't the bulls fighting each other. It's ... people fighting the bulls."

"But that's surely very dangerous? And very foolish?" said Uncle Otto. "Bulls are stronger, and have horns."

So Con tried to explain. "It's a sort of sport. They choose a very strong, fierce bull and lead him into the bullring, which is a huge place a bit like a football stadium. And there are these people called picadors, who ride horses and have spears to jab into the bull and make him angry. And then some other people called banderilleros come and stick arrows into the bull's neck and then when he's very tired, the top bloke, who's called a matador, makes him charge and kills him with his sword."

There was a long silence while the yetis looked at him.

"*People* do that?" said Ambrose at last. "Proper human people?"

Con nodded miserably.

The yetis didn't say anything. But one by one they went up to their bunks and shut their ear lids and turned their faces to the wall. They wanted to have nothing to do with Santa Maria, not even to *see* a place where things like that were done.

After crawling along for another few hundred metres, Perry gave up. People had come in from all the surrounding countryside to see the fight and had just parked their cars and motorbikes and farm carts anywhere they could find, jamming up the roads completely.

"We'll have to wait till it's over," he said, "and people move their stuff."

So he drew up under a poster which announced that this very afternoon, Pedro the Passionate, the most famous matador in Spain, was going to fight El Magnifico, the fiercest bull ever to be bred on the ranches of Pamplona. And when he had convinced Con that the *Mutter*-shouting girl was not likely to turn up with her parents six hundred miles from where they'd left her, he took him and Ellen to a pavement café and they had ice cream and watched the streets empty as everyone was drawn, as if by a gigantic magnet, towards the bullring in the central square.

Meanwhile, back in the lorry, Hubert was feeling lonely and neglected. The yetis were still lying on their bunks with their faces to the wall. Nobody loved him. Nobody *cared*.

His boot face began to crumple. He threw back his head, ready to bleat.

And then he stopped. He had heard a voice. An incredible voice, deep and thrilling and purple. Not a moo. Something stronger than a moo. More of a roar.

Could it be...?

But no, it didn't sound *quite* like his mother.

The noise came again. A low, throbbing sort of bellow. And suddenly Hubert knew what it was. Something even more exciting than his mother. Something he'd had long ago and forgotten all about.

The thing that was making that noise – was Hubert's *father*!

It took Hubert some time to push up the iron bar which closed the back of the lorry, but butting steadily with his little crumpled horn, he did it. The yetis had dozed off with their ear lids closed. No one noticed Hubert jump down, trot across the deserted square and reach the edge of the bullring.

It was made of wooden palings, high and solid and unclimbable. But Hubert didn't mean to climb. Puffing with excitement, he trotted round it looking for a soft place in the ground.

From inside, the bellow came again, filling the whole square with its power.

Hubert hesitated no longer. There was a small gap in the wooden railing patched with canvas, and beside it a pile of rubble where a new water pipe went underground. A perfect Hubert Hole. And putting down his battered head, the little yak began to dig.

The bull they called El Magnifico stood alone in the centre of the ring. Sweat gleamed on the huge hump of muscle which ran down his back; his eyes were wide with terror; blood streamed from a wound in his flank.

A few days ago he had roamed free on the range, feeling the wind between his horns, the good grass beneath his feet. Then men had come and carted him away and kept him for two days in a darkened pen. And now he'd been pushed, half blinded, into this place where men rushed at him on horses and others leaped at him with arrows, and everywhere there were flickering red cloths, and the screams of the crowd, and pain and fear.

But El Magnifico was a great bull. He did not understand why these things were being done to him but he would fight to the end. And he lowered his head and pawed the ground and when the prancing men came with their arrows, he charged.

"Olé!" yelled the crowd. And "Aah!" as a

banderillero vaulted to safety over the barrier.

But the bull was growing tired. One of the banderillero's arrows had pierced the muscles of his throat. Soon Pedro the Passionate would provoke him to the charge that would be his last.

"Kill!" roared the crowd to Pedro the Passionate. "Kill the bull! Kill! Kill! Kill!"

Wretched, exhausted, scenting his own death, the great bull lifted his head in a last bellow of misery and pain.

The bellow was answered. Not by an answering *roar* exactly. By a small but very happy bleat. And then the yak called Hubert tottered on his spindly legs into the ring.

He was covered in sawdust and rubble, his left horn looked like a toy corkscrew and a piece of water pipe, dislodged by his tunnelling, had caught in his tail.

Ignoring the murmurs of the crowd, not even *seeing* the picadors on their skinny horses

or the prancing banderilleros with their arrows or Pedro the Passionate standing open-mouthed, his cape in his hand, Hubert tottered forward. Only one thing existed for him: El Magnifico the bull.

"Father!" said Hubert in yak language. "Daddy! It's your son. It's me!"

El Magnifico was completely taken by surprise. He stopped bellowing and pawing and charging and bent his head to look at whatever it was that was blissfully butting him from underneath. He didn't *think* he had a calf like that. His calves, as far as he remembered, were larger and smoother and had a different smell. But with fifty wives one could never be sure. And slowly El Magnifico put out his huge, rough tongue and carefully, painstakingly, began to lick Hubert into shape.

Hubert had never been so happy. No one had licked him since he'd left Nanvi Dar. He trembled with joy, he squeaked with pleasure, he rolled over on his back...

"Aah! The sweet little one," sighed the women in the crowd.

Pedro the Passionate was furious. There are rules about bullfighting like there are rules about boxing. You can't just go up to the back end of a bull and stick him in the behind. To earn his money, Pedro had to *make* him charge.

So he flicked his fingers and the picadors on their poor, skinny horses tried to ride up to El Magnifico again and jab him with their spears and make him fight.

But they had reckoned without the horses. A pawing, stamping bull was their enemy – but a father licking his son was a different matter. They, too, had had foals in distant and happy days before they were sold off to be ripped to pieces in the ring. At first they just wouldn't budge however much the picadors jabbed them with their spears. And then, to show they meant business – the horses sat down.

After that the audience went mad. The men rolled about in their seats laughing. The women took out their handkerchiefs and began to sob, because it was all so touching and beautiful.

But Pedro the Passionate nearly exploded with rage. He was being turned into a laughing stock. He *had* to kill the bull. He *had* to show them.

So angry was he that he felt no fear, but pranced right up to the bull and flicked him with his cape. Anything to make him charge.

El Magnifico didn't even notice. He was working on a particularly difficult place behind Hubert's right ear. But Hubert had seen the cape: a nasty, swirling thing it was, and it made him nervous. With a worried bleat he rushed forward – right between Pedro the Passionate's velvet trouser legs.

And the last bullfight of the season ended with the mightiest matador in Spain lying flat on his back in the sawdust, a pram-sized yak nibbling the bobbles of his embroidered waistcoat – and the fiercest bull ever bred in Pamplona licking them both.

10

Farley Towers

Bulls who have not been killed in the ring are never used again for fights. So the next day, El Magnifico was sent back by special train to the ranch from which he had come: a beautiful place with fresh, green grass, chestnut groves and cool breezes from the mountains of Navarre. And with him travelled his adopted son, an animal that had become famous throughout Spain – the yak called Hubert.

It was this ranch, in the hills above Pamplona, to which, on a moonlit night a couple of days later, the yellow lorry travelled. Perry had found out where the bull had been taken and they had broken their journey to the coast to say goodbye.

When the yetis had woken up to find Hubert gone, their distress had been terrible.

"I didn't look after him properly," Ambrose had wailed over and over again. "I didn't deserve to have a yak of my own."

"Do you remember his little hooves?" Lucy sobbed. "Just like mother-of-pearl, they were."

"And the clatter of his knees knocking together. I can hear it now," Grandma had moaned.

But now they were trying to be brave.

"After all, every growing person needs a father," said sensible Uncle Otto.

"Look how we miss ours," said Lucy, choking back a burst of tears.

"That El Magnifico animal will be the making of him, I daresay," said Grandma.

But Ambrose didn't say anything. Being brave was beyond him as he faced a yak-less world.

About a mile from the ranch, Perry parked the lorry and while Con went ahead to see that the coast was clear, the yetis crept silently across the fields towards the paddock which housed El Magnifico and his new son.

There had been clouds over the moon, but as they came up to the railings they rolled past and in a shaft of silver light they saw their yak, lying like a shaggy mop-head against the vast flanks of the sleeping bull.

"Hubert!" said Ambrose in a deep and tragic voice. "Are you happy, Hubert? Is this what you wanted?"

Hubert scrambled to his feet and ran forward to the railings. His boot face quivered with excitement, his knock knees clattered together like castanets. Here was Ambrose the Abominable, here were his old friends! He began to butt the railings, making little slivers of sawdust with his crumpled horn.

El Magnifico didn't move. He just lifted his great head, with the wide and curving horns, and waited.

It was a terrible moment. The yetis could have picked Hubert up with one hand and lifted him over the fence and that would have been that. But Lady Agatha had brought them up well. They knew that people – even very young ones like Hubert – have to make their own choices.

So they waited, while Hubert ran backwards and forwards, now butting El Magnifico in the stomach, now rushing back to the railings to stick his nose into Ambrose's outstretched hand.

For a moment it looked as though old loyalties would be the strongest. Hubert even put his head down and started tunnelling a path under the railings. Then with a last bleat of confusion, he stopped, turned and collapsed against the great bull's side.

It was over. Fatherhood had won.

After that, no one tried to be brave any more. Though Con and Ellen travelled in the back to try and console the yetis, there was little they could do. Lucy sat clutching Hubert's rubber teat while her blonde stomach turned dark under a rain of tears. Grandma said they needn't expect her to get over a grief like that at her age and Clarence, managing a whole word for once, said, "Gone," over and over again in a deep and desperate voice. As for Ambrose the Abominable, he lay like a felled log on his bunk, his wall eyes fixed blankly on the ceiling, brokenly murmuring Hubert's name.

After a few miles, Perry stopped the lorry. He needed a short sleep before the last lap which would take them to the vehicle ferry. So he switched off the engine, bent down to pick up his pipe and settled back in his seat. Dawn was just breaking, a pale streak of light on the horizon.

Perry took a puff at his pipe. Then suddenly he leaned forward and peered into the driving mirror.

After that he used Bad Language. Then he looked into the mirror again to make sure that he had seen what he thought he had seen.

He had.

For a moment, Perry was tempted. It would have been so easy to start the engine, release the handbrake, let out the clutch and take off at full speed down the road. Then he sighed, got down and opened the back of the lorry.

So then they all saw what Perry had seen in the driving mirror.

Footsore, knock-kneed, tripping over the tufts of hair that hung from his chest and bleating a frantic, "wait-for-me" bleat – came Hubert.

The yetis being sad had been hard to bear but the yetis being happy was almost as exhausting. By the time the lorry drove into the bowels of the big, white ship that was to take them across to Britain, Con and Ellen were quite worn out.

"I do hope they'll be quiet during the crossing," said Con. "I hate to lock them in – it seems so rude – but with the ship so full, I think we'll have to."

But Con needn't have worried. He could have left the door wide open and none of the yetis would have stirred a centimetre. And the reason for this was simple – they were seasick.

There is always a rough patch of water round the Bay of Biscay and as the boat began to heave and toss, the yetis, unused as they were to the sea, became hideously, horribly, vilely ill. Grandma lay in her bunk groaning and saying that since the ship was going to sink anyway she hoped it would sink *quickly*. Lucy swore that she would never again say "sorry" to so much as a peanut if only her stomach would come out of the back of her throat and go back to where it belonged, and Ambrose, his head in a plastic bucket, was trying to decide who should have his bedsock when he was dead.

There is little you can do for people who are seasick except leave them alone. So while Perry sat in the bar drinking all the beer he hadn't been able to drink while he was driving, Con and Ellen, who were good sailors, stayed up on deck watching the white spray and the diving gulls and the green wake of their ship in the water. And gradually, as they approached the shores of England, a weight seemed to fall off Con's back, because it looked as though he had really done what he had promised Lady Agatha, and brought the yetis safely to her home.

They landed at Southampton two days later and while the exhausted yetis dozed in the back, Perry set course for the village of Farlingham, now only a couple of hours' drive away.

It was a gentle, misty morning and as they drove past quiet fields and bird-busy hedges, past little copses and peaceful villages, they thought – as people do when they come back to the place where they were born – that there was nowhere quite like it in the world.

"Have you ever thought," said Perry, when they stopped at a transport café for some fish and chips, "that Farley Towers may not be there any more? That it's been pulled down to make a motorway or some such thing? Or that the people who own it have sold it to a hotel or a school or something?"

"I've thought of it often," said Con. "But I don't

see what to do except hope for the best."

All the same, when Perry turned off by a signpost saying "Farlingham 2 miles", Con could have cried with relief. For there, at the end of a most beautiful avenue of lime trees was the house which Lady Agatha had described to him, weeks and weeks ago, in the secret valley of Nanvi Dar.

Lady Agatha had not been exaggerating. It really was one of the loveliest houses he had ever seen. Bathed in sunlight, its mellow brick glowed softly. There were wide inviting terraces which fell away to the rolling meadows of the deer park with its ancient elms. Yellow water lilies studded the lake, and on the wrought-iron gates the Farlingham crest shone proudly.

"All the same, I'll just check at the village shop," said Con. "Make sure the Farlinghams are still there."

So he went into the village shop, which was the old-fashioned kind with sweets in glass jars, and liquorice and bootlaces and apples all jumbled up on the counter. Con bought a quarter of Black Bullets and then, trying to keep his voice casual, he asked who the big house belonged to.

"Oh, that's the Farlinghams' place," said the woman behind the till. "Been in the family since way back."

"Are they nice people?" said Con.

"None nicer," said the shop lady. "I reckon there's no one would have a bad word to say for the Farlinghams. Which is more than you can say for some of these old families."

"Well, I guess we're home and dry then," said Perry when Con came back. "If they don't clap me in jail, that is, for turning in an empty lorry. It's the Perrington Porker for me and back to Bukhim for the two of you, I guess."

Con nodded. "I'd like just to see them safely into Farley Towers, though."

"Of course," said Perry. "Tell you what, I'll book a room for tonight in the pub here. The Farlinghams will probably want you and Ellen to stay with them, but I'd rather be independent. Then tomorrow I can get up to town and see the Cold Carcass people and book your flight home. OK?"

"OK," said Con, and he went to tell the yetis that they had arrived.

When he opened the door of the lorry, he had quite a surprise. Ellen, who had been travelling in the back with them, had worked really hard. Their fur shone, Queen Victoria glistened with polish between the shining plaits on Lucy's stomach and the bedsock was arranged across Ambrose's burnished chest like the Order of the Garter.

"Aren't we smart!" said Ambrose the Abominable. "They'll like us like this, won't they, at Farley Towers?"

"They'd better," said Con in a gruff voice. He'd just begun to understand what it would be like to go back to Bukhim and not see the yetis any more.

And seeing the yetis look so smart made the children suddenly realize how crumpled and dishevelled they themselves were looking after the long journey. You can brush fur, but you can't do much about missing buttons and torn jumpers and socks with holes in them.

"Look, now we know the Farlinghams are still there, I think you should go ahead," said Con to the yetis. "After all, you're sort of family from having been brought up by Lady Agatha, and you've got the bedsock to show who you are. We'll find a field to put Hubert in and then we'll go with Perry to his pub and clean ourselves up and then we'll join you. All right?"

The yetis nodded. "But you'll come *soon*, won't you?" said Ambrose, managing to keep his voice wobble free, but only just.

"Very soon," promised Con.

But when the yetis set off up the avenue of lime trees that led, wide and straight and welcoming, from the main gateway of Farley Towers to the house, they couldn't feel shy and nervous any more. It was so lovely to walk upright and unashamed without being afraid to be seen. Not that there was anyone about in the deserted park, but if there had been it wouldn't have mattered because they were safe now, they *belonged*.

"'ice!" said Clarence in a pleased voice, looking about him.

"Yes, *isn't* it nice?" said Lucy. "It's just like walking into the Farley Towers game. Look, there's the lake where we're going to row and have picnics with lemonade."

"And there's the summer house where Lady Agatha used to read Beautiful Poetry," said Grandma.

"If only she could be with us now. And Father too!" sighed Uncle Otto.

They walked on steadily up the long, curiously empty drive between the lime trees, which made an arch above their heads, and came out on the wide sweep of gravel in front of the great, iron-studded door.

"They will be our friends and tell us stories?" said Ambrose, suddenly feeling rather wobbly and scared.

"Of course they will," said Grandma. "Now come on, ring the bell."

And bravely, Ambrose the Abominable took off his bedsock and, holding it carefully in his right hand, he pulled the big brass handle of the bell. They could hear it peal in the back of the huge house – a deep, long peal. There were footsteps, a creak as of a metal bar being pulled back – and then the great front door swung open and the yetis went inside.

The long journey was over. They were home.

11

The Hunter's Club

While the yetis were walking up the long drive to Farley Towers, a meeting was being held inside the house, in the Gold drawing room, which faced the rose gardens and the terrace at the back.

The Gold drawing room looked much as it had looked in Lady Agatha's day. The beautiful Chinese vases were still there, and the embroidered screen and the harpsichord. The sacred relic was there too: the *other* bedsock, the one that the Earl had brought back from Nanvi Dar and slept with under his pillow until he died.

But there were other things now, hung on the walls or resting on the furniture: things which would never have been allowed in the house when Lady Agatha was a girl. Heads they were, mostly. The stuffed heads of friendly hippopotamuses and gentle giraffes and thoughtful buffaloes, looking down on the room with sad and glassy eyes. There were skins, too – the skins of slaughtered tigers and zebras and leopards lying on top of the lovely, flower-patterned carpet. Sawn-off tusks and antlers were piled above the mantlepiece and in a glass case the bodies of poor, dead fishes hung stiffly.

The meeting was a big one. There were about thirty people sitting round a huge satinwood table, all of them men. And not one of them was a Farlingham.

The lady in the shop had not been lying when she said that Farley Towers still belonged to the Farlinghams. It did. But like many old families, the Farlinghams had become poor. They couldn't afford any longer to keep the acres of roof mended, or pay gardeners to tend the grounds, or servants to care for the ninety-seven rooms. So they had decided to let the house to a school or a club or a hospital who would be able to look after it. And their agent, who looked after things for them, *had* let it to a club. A club that wanted to move from its headquarters in London to a place in the country because it needed more room.

The Hunter's Club, it was called...

The members of the Hunter's Club came from all over the world. There were oil sheiks from Iran, film stars from Hollywood, German industrialists, Spanish noblemen – anyone who thought that killing defenceless animals turned you into a "real" man. It cost twenty thousand pounds just to *join* the club and the funds were used to buy aeroplanes and motorboats and snowmobiles so that members could go and kill even the rarest animals in the most distant places without anyone being able to stop them.

In this way the Hunters had gunned down polar bears on the icebergs of Alaska, practically exterminated the Javan rhinoceroses and massacred the gentle, dreamy orang-utans of Borneo. Sometimes they went off on pig-sticking parties in Spain, running wild boars through with spears as they quietly snuffled under the chestnut trees, or they would fly to some African lake and mow down hundreds of gorgeous flamingoes from the comfort of their jeeps.

"Now then, gentlemen," said the club president, a man called Colonel Bagwackerly, who had a boiled-looking face, pop eyes and a sticky moustache which clung like a slice of ginger pudding to his face. "As you know, we are here to discuss a very important matter."

"A very important matter!" yelled the Hunters, banging their glasses on the table. They were already rather drunk.

"As you know," Bagwackerly went on, "next week our great club is going to be one hundred years old."

"One hundred years old!" repeated the Hunters, hiccuping and slapping each other on the back.

"And we are here to decide what kind of hunt we should have for our anniversary celebrations."

"A big hunt! The biggest hunt ever!" cried the drunken Hunters.

"Quite so," said Bagwackerly. "The only question is, what shall we hunt. And where?"

"How about polishing off the rest of the blue whales?" said a black-bearded Scotsman who called himself the MacDermot-Duff of Huist and Carra, and went around in a blood-red kilt and a sporran hung with a dozen dangling badger's claws.

But the others shook their heads. Not enough sport, they said, and it was true. So many of these rare and marvellous animals had already been destroyed by greedy whale hunters that you could travel a thousand miles across the ice-blue waters of the Antarctic and not sight one.

"Vat if ve go schtick-pigging?" said a German member, Herr Blutenstein from Hamburg. But the others shook their heads again. For a big centenary hunt they wanted something bigger than pig-sticking; something with guns in it, and explosions, and blood.

One member suggested a kangaroo shoot in Australia, but so many of the kangaroos had already been turned into steaks that that wasn't any good. Someone else suggested the wild camels in the Andes, but a revolution was going on in South America and the Hunters liked shooting things, not getting shot.

And then a small man with gold-rimmed spectacles and a pinched, pale nose got to his feet.

"I know!" he squeaked. "I know! I've got a great idea!"

"What is it, Prink?" said Colonel Bagwackerly in a weary voice.

They had let Mr Prink belong to the club because he was a very rich saucepan manufacturer and they needed him to buy helicopters and things like that. But everyone despised him: he was weedy and twittery and had a huge wife called Myrtle Prink of whom he was dreadfully afraid.

Now he tried to jump on his chair, fell off and

squeaked: "Yetis! That's what we should hunt! Abominable Snowmen! Fly out to the Himalayas and have a great big yeti hunt!"

There were groans from the other Hunters and the MacDermot-Duff of Huish and Carra swore a dreadful oath. "Don't be an imbecile, Prink," he said. "There aren't any such things."

"Yes, there are, there are!" shouted Mr Prink. "Look!"

And he took out a bundle of newspapers and threw them down on the table.

They were the papers that had been printed after Lucy's footsteps had been found on Nanvi Dar and the headlines said things like: ABOMINABLE SNOWMAN STALKS AGAIN or MYSTERIOUS DENIZENS OF THE MOUNTAIN HEIGHTS or IT'S YES TO THE YETIS.

"Pull yourself together, Prink," snarled Bagwackerly. "A pack of newspaper lies."

"It isn't, I'm sure it isn't," squealed Mr Prink. "We could stalk them in the snow and flush them from their lairs and shoot them with exploding bullets. We could have a yeti skin for the billiard room and yeti tusks in the armoury and—"

"Ein yeti schkalp für die library!" shouted Herr Blutenstein from Hamburg.

"That's *enough*!" thundered Colonel Bagwackerly. "If I hear another word about yetis, Prink, I'll have you thrown out of the club." He broke off. "Drat it, that's the doorbell, and I had to send the servants away. Can't have them prying into our affairs. Go and see who it is, Prink, you might as well do something useful for once."

So Mr Prink got up and went out of the room. When he came back, he couldn't speak. His mouth opened, his mouth shut, but that was all.

"Well, what is it?" said Bagwackerly impatiently. "Who was there?"

"It's ... it's ... what you said I mustn't say another word about," stammered Mr Prink. "With ... bedsocks."

Furiously, Bagwackerly pushed him aside and strode out into the hall. When he came back his bloated face looked as though it had been dipped in flour. "My God," he said, groping to loosen his tie, "my God..."

And then, with a great effort, he pulled himself together. "Shut the door, quickly, quickly," he said. "We've only got a couple of minutes. We must make a plan."

The yetis were sitting in the Blue salon having

afternoon tea. They were sitting very close together though the room was vast – so close that Ambrose and Lucy could curl their seventh toes together like they used to do when they were small.

Polite afternoon tea is not an easy meal for yetis. When they balanced the fragile teacups on their knees, the cups sank right into their fur and couldn't easily be found again, and the biscuits were so thin that they had to say, "Sorry, biscuit," about ten times before they got a mouthful.

But that wasn't why they were sitting so close together. They were sitting like that because of the things on the walls. Lady Agatha had not told them about the things that would be on the walls of the Blue salon and the Gold drawing room and all the other rooms that the yetis had seen. Right above Ambrose, so that his trunk almost dipped into Ambrose's teacup, was the head of a poor, dead elephant. Grandma was sitting next to a large stuffed marabou and Uncle Otto's bald patch had two nasty scratches where a pair of moose antlers had caught him as he bent forward to pass the jam.

And though Lady Agatha's relations had been very nice to them, somehow they had not been quite like the yetis expected. The one with the red face and the gingery moustache who said he was Uncle George had such strange pop eyes and when he spoke it made the yetis feel that they were soldiers on parade rather than members of the family. Uncle Mac, who came from Scotland, had sworn quite dreadfully when he had spilt some hot water on his bare and tufty knees, and though the yetis were used to Bad Language from when Perry changed a wheel, somehow this was different. As for Uncle Leslie, he was such a twitchy, squeaky little man that he made the yetis very nervous. There didn't seem to be any women in the family either, which was a pity. A woman's touch would perhaps have made them feel more welcome.

"'ump," said Clarence sadly. He meant the lump of sugar which, for the third time, had dropped from the sugar tongs on to the carpet.

"I wish Con and Ellen would come," whispered Ambrose – and it was rather an uncertain whisper. "They promised to say goodbye to us."

"Another cup of tea?" asked Uncle George.

But the yetis said, thank you, they had had enough.

"Come, come, just one more cup, I insist. Prink – er, Uncle Leslie, another cup for our visitors. For our *relations*, I should say."

So Uncle Leslie poured out another five cups of tea, keeping his back turned to the yetis, and then Uncle George leaned over and dropped a small, white pill into each of them.

"Let us drink to your happy stay with us," he said.

The yetis were far too polite to refuse a toast. They hadn't wanted any more tea but now, one by one, they tilted their cups into their mouths and drank.

"That ... poor elephant's ... all... swelled up," said Ambrose groggily.

"I feel funny," whispered Lucy. "Not nice funny: nasty funny."

For a moment longer, the poor, drugged yetis struggled against unconsciousness. Then there was a crash as Uncle Otto fell forward across the tea things. Grandma slid off the sofa and came to rest in a grey and crumpled heap on the Persian carpet. Poor, bewildered Clarence keeled over sideways, taking a case of stuffed pike with him as he fell. Then Lucy and Ambrose collapsed into each other's arms – and it was over.

It is easy to trick innocent creatures who trust you. The yetis would not wake for a long time now. And when they did, the fate in store for them was too dreadful for anyone to imagine.

An hour later, Con and Ellen walked up the long avenue of lime trees towards the iron-studded door of Farley Towers.

The grounds were surprisingly deserted. No gardeners bent over the flower beds, no strollers enjoying the golden afternoon.

"Look, an aeroplane! A big one!"

Con tilted his head back at the plane which had appeared suddenly, rising steeply from the fields behind the house. The Farlinghams must have their own airstrip! The thought that they were going to visit people rich and grand enough to run their own aeroplanes made the children rather nervous. They had done their best, pulling the last of their clean clothes out of the battered holdall, but they still weren't exactly smart.

"I'm glad we didn't bring Hubert," said Ellen.

Perry, who wanted to get to the pub for opening time, had lifted Hubert over a low fence into a field of cows. They were the very *best* cows, pedigree Jerseys with soft doe eyes, but Hubert had just turned his back on them and started grazing. After having a famous father like El Magnifico he didn't seem to be interested in mothers any more.

They had reached the gravelled space in front of the house. For a moment they hesitated. The Farlinghams would probably ask them to stay the night, but after that it was goodbye to the yetis, and both the children had lumps in their throats when they thought of it.

"Come on," said Con, "let's get it over," and he ran up the wide flight of steps, and rang the bell.

For a long time, nobody came. Then there were footsteps: slow, heavy ones, and the door was creakingly pulled back.

The first thing the children saw, almost at eye level, was a pair of bony knees with black tufts of hair on them. Then, travelling upwards, they came to a blood-red kilt, a sporran with dangling badger's claws and – much, much higher – a black beard and glittering black eyes...

"Yes," snapped the bearded Scotsman.

"I'm Con Bellamy. This is my sister, Ellen. We've come to see that the yetis are all right and to say goodbye to them. Lady Agatha asked us to—"

"Yetis," snarled the man. "What are you talking about?"

"The yetis who came just now. Ambrose and the others."

"Look, if you're having a joke with me you've chosen the wrong person," said the man. "Yetis, my foot. Now get along both of you. This is a respectable stately home and we don't want any guttersnipes cluttering it up."

"But they *must* be here," said Con desperately.

"Perhaps—" And then he jumped back as the great oak door was slammed in his face.

Feeling suddenly sick with fear, the children turned and went slowly down the steps.

"What *can* have happened?" said Ellen. "Can they have got lost?"

"Hardly, down a dead straight avenue. Maybe Ambrose found a friend?"

But what sort of a friend? Not only were there no people about in the grounds, there were no animals either. No dogs sniffed the moist earth, no cats climbed the rooftops. Even the rooks in the elm trees seemed to have fled.

"Perhaps they've gone to explore the lake or something?"

"We'd better have a look, anyway."

So, fighting down their panic, they searched the woods around the lake, and the Greek temple, and the kitchen gardens behind their sheltering walls. They searched the banks of the stream and the orchard and the stables but there was no sign of the yetis anywhere.

They were searching the topiary, with its yew trees cut into all sorts of shapes, when they saw a second plane come up from behind the house and fly off towards the south.

"There's something very wrong with this..." began Con. Then he broke off. "What is it, Ellen?"

His sister was standing stock still with her hands over her face. He went over to her. Lying at her feet was a cat – an ordinary, tortoiseshell cat.

It had been shot clean through the heart.

For a moment, neither of them could speak. Then: "I'm going to break in," said Con. "I'm going to get into the house *somehow*. Come on, let's try the back."

At first it seemed to be hopeless. The hundred or so windows were tightly shut; the green-painted doors were bolted. And then Con saw one narrow window on the ground floor where the catch had not been pushed completely across the frame. Carefully, levering with his penknife, Con started to work the wood away from the sill. It came slowly, but it came. And then they had climbed through and dropped down safely inside Farley Towers.

They were in the butler's pantry. There was silver waiting to be polished, striped aprons lying on the chair, a big sink... Silently pushing open the green baize door they crept along the stone corridor which connected the servants' quarters with the main part of the house.

There were no footsteps to be heard, no sound of voices. Farley Towers seemed to be totally deserted.

And then, as they reached the hallway which led to the main back door, they stopped with a gasp.

Lying like a blue stain across the flagstones – was Ambrose's bedsock.

"So the man was telling lies. The yetis *have* been here," said Con.

But Ellen had noticed something else. "Look, there's Grandma's shawl, all crumpled up behind that chest. And Queen Victoria..."

"They've been *stripped*," said Con, his teeth beginning to chatter. "Someone has—"

He was stopped by a cry. A weird, strangled, spluttering cry from somewhere below them. "Hublopp!" it sounded like. "Blumph. Haroo!"

"It's coming from the cellar," said Ellen.

They opened one door to a cupboard, another to a lumber room. Then they found it – a dusty, wooden door from which a flight of dank, stone steps led downwards. And there, between cobwebby barrels, the thing that had been making the noises writhed and wriggled.

Con wrenched the gag from its mouth. It was Mr Prink, whom the other Hunters had gagged and bound and thrown into the cellar.

"What's happened?" said Con. "Who did this? *Where are the yetis?*"

Mr Prink became hysterical. "It was just because they talked that I didn't want to join in the shoot. I've never shot anything that talked," he gabbled. "If I'd been able to shoot anything that talked I'd have shot Mrs Prink. Mrs Prink is my wife and she makes me eat mashed potatoes with lumps in them—"

"Shut up about Mrs Prink. What's happened to the yetis?"

"They're on a plane, on the way to the ice floes. There's going to be a great hunt down there in the Antarctic."

Con steadied himself. It was no good giving in to panic now.

"Why there? Why ice floes?"

"So they can run better. They want some sport, you know. This is the famous Hunter's Club. It's no fun shooting animals that just stand still. And everyone in England's so namby-pamby. You can't shoot this, you can't kill that."

"When is this hunt going to start?"

"On Thursday. It's for the centenary of the Hunter's Club. They're all going to fly out and chase them in snowmobiles. The only yetis in the world and all for the club. Yeti skins," raved Mr Prink, "yeti antlers, yeti tusks!"

Con kicked him. "Shut up, you murdering brute. Where exactly are they being dropped?"

"I can't tell you— Ow! Ow! You're hurting me!"

"If you don't tell me I won't hurt you, I'll kill you," said Con, and he meant it.

"A place called Coldwater Straits, near Smithson Island. It's really good hunting country because there's nowhere for them to hide. And I wanted to go too. But I've never shot anything that talked. If I'd been able to shoot anything that talked I'd have shot my wife. Mrs Prink is not a nice woman. She makes me take castor oil even when I'm regular and—"

Con wanted to put his thumbs against Mr Prink's jugular vein and press hard, but there was one more thing he wanted to know.

"How did they make the yetis go with them? What lies did they tell?"

Mr Prink giggled. "They didn't. They put drugs in their tea. And I wanted to go with them, I did really, but I've never shot anything that talked. I've shot a very big rhinoceros from an armour-plated Land Rover, but it didn't talk. If I'd been able to shoot anything that talked I'd have shot Mrs— Help! Help! Where are you going? You've got to untie me!"

"Not a chance," said Con.

It was only when they got out into the fresh air that the real horror of what they'd heard hit the children and then they just clung together in shock, unable to speak.

"It's Monday today, isn't it?" said Con when he could manage words again.

Ellen nodded. On Thursday a plane load of crazy men would set off for Coldwater Straits to murder the yetis.

They had three days to stop them. To achieve the impossible. Just three short days.

12

Coldwater Straits

When the yetis woke they were in the bleakest, most terrible place you could imagine. All around them, stretching to the horizon, was a flat plain of snow and ice, broken only by low ridges like ragged teeth, and here and there a huge frozen block. There was no trace of colour, no blade of grass, no living thing as far as the eye could see – only the shrill screaming of the wind across the sunless waste.

"Oh, where are we? What has happened to us?" cried Ambrose, who was the first to come round after the drugs.

One by one the yetis came to, and stared with wretchedness at the place to which they had been brought.

"I can't remember anything after we drank those cups of tea with the Farlingham uncles," said Lucy.

"Why have they sent us here?" said Grandma. "This place isn't fit for a worm."

"They can't have *meant* to," said Ambrose wretchedly. "Unless we've been bad. Was it our table manners?"

"Pack ice," mused Uncle Otto. "The North Pole? The South Pole? Alaska...?"

"I don't want to be in a pole," wailed Ambrose. "I want Con and Ellen. I want—"

But Lucy had discovered something even more serious. "There's nothing to eat here," she said. "Absolutely nothing."

It was true. Nothing grew on that frozen desert – no moss, no lichen, no grass.

"Wait a minute," said Grandma. "What are those black and white chickens over there?"

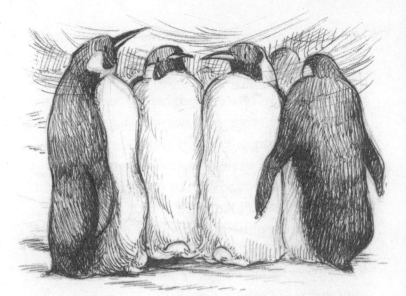

"The penguins, do you mean?" said Uncle Otto.

"We can't eat *them*," said Ambrose, shocked. "They're our brothers."

"Don't be silly," said Grandma, "Of course we can't eat *flesh*. But maybe they've laid some eggs."

So they made their way slowly and painfully across the ice, doubled up against the wind. It was dreadfully hard going. The surface looked smooth from a distance, but in fact it was rough, and sharp where floes had been cast on edge by the wind before freezing into the solid mass. The yetis' poor backward-pointing feet were soon bruised and torn.

And it was unbelievably cold. Yetis can stand almost any amount of cold, but this was beyond anything they had ever experienced. The wind whipped the heat out of their faces and hands, and even the almost impenetrable yeti hair was not enough to keep them warm. Soon they were freezing as they had never frozen in their mountain home.

And when they got up to the silent huddle of penguins it was all no good. It's true each of the birds had an egg balanced between its red, webbed toes. But one egg only. *The* egg.

"Sorry, penguin's egg," said Lucy, who was really unbearably hungry.

Then she looked at the father bird standing there quite quietly, not squawking, not protesting, just *suffering,* and she choked and turned away.

"I can't do it," said Lucy. "It's his Little One. It's the only one he's got."

In the lovely, fertile valley of Nanvi Dar, which now seemed just like a distant dream to the yetis, Lady Agatha had taught them always to say "sorry" to only one egg in a nest, so as to leave plenty for the mother bird. But of course in Nanvi Dar there had been no penguins.

Though it had never been properly light, it now became darker and the yetis clung to one another for warmth and comfort. Grandma and Uncle Otto, who were old and experienced, were beginning to give up hope, but for the sake of the children they pretended to believe in rescue. "We must keep moving," said Uncle Otto. "This is polar pack ice. There must be land we can walk to and find some kind of shelter, a cave perhaps. And we will be easier to spot if we are on the move."

"That's right," said Grandma, "and when an aeroplane comes we must shout and wave our arms so they'll see us."

"An aeroplane *will* come, won't it?" said Ambrose. "With Con and Ellen in it?"

"Of course it will," said Uncle Otto. "There has just been some silly mistake."

"What sort of mistake?" asked Ambrose.

"Oh, I expect they wanted to give us a treat so they..." But even Uncle Otto couldn't think of a convincing explanation of how they had come by accident to this ghastly place.

So they started to walk, forcing themselves forward through the gathering darkness, while the wind tore at them, their breath froze and formed icicles in their eyebrows and nostrils and a deathly cold crept slowly but surely through their thick coats, and into their very bones.

After what seemed like many hours of struggling over the treacherous surface, Clarence stopped.

"'oise," he said.

And now the others heard what he had heard.

"An aeroplane," croaked Ambrose. "I knew Con would come." But it was far too dark now for an aeroplane to be out looking for them. It was a strange sound, unlike any they had heard before. It was a deep groaning and creaking, as though some huge monster was turning in an unquiet sleep.

Now Uncle Otto felt despair overwhelming him, for he realized what had happened. Instead of heading for land, the yetis had gone in the wrong direction, and had come to the very edge of the Antarctic ice pack, and what they heard was the sea beating against it, driving new floes into it, breaking others off, sometimes gaining ground, sometimes retreating as the temperature dropped and the sea froze a bit more.

But before Otto could warn the yetis of the terrible danger they were in, there was a sudden booming noise. It was a terrifying sound like the striking of a vast gong under their feet, and the shocked yetis saw a crack open and come rushing towards them, widening all the time. They leaped aside in a panic.

"We must turn back," cried Uncle Otto. They did turn back, wearily struggling over the torn and twisted ice, but they didn't get very far. Utterly exhausted, at the end of their endurance, they collapsed into a miserable huddle, pressing close to one another to preserve a tiny bit of warmth. They could go no further.

As the long polar night dragged on, the yetis told each other stories. They told each other all the gentlest, funniest stories, because they didn't feel like too much adventure. Stories about Mole and Ratty in *The Wind in the Willows* and about Alice and the Mock Turtle and about Henry King who had Swallowed Little Bits of String. And at last, wretched as they were, they fell asleep.

But then a terrible thing happened. Lucy had stopped sleepwalking on the journey from Nanvi Dar. It is a thing you grow out of, like adenoids or sucking your thumb. But now, in her misery and fear, she got up, stretched out her arms and began to totter – eyes open but unseeing – across the cruel ice towards the sea.

She did not get far. A dark gash opened in front of her. There was a splash – a terrible one, like a submerging tank – and then Lucy, who could not swim a stroke, was sucked down into the icy, heaving waters of the coldest seas in the world.

There would have been no hope for her. But though the land of the Antarctic is the most desolate place in the world, there are animals in the sea. And it so happened that two leopard seals had come up to breathe not far away. And when those kind and sensible animals saw that the thing that had fallen into the water was not making the right sort of movements at all – was, in fact, sinking like a stone – they quickly went to help.

It was a hard job, but heaving and buffeting and shoving they managed to edge Lucy's huge bulk on to the ice again.

It was there that the others found her in the morning. A human would have died very quickly. To get wet is the worst thing that can happen to you in those conditions (even sweating in your protective clothing is dangerous) and Lucy was soaked to the skin. But Lucy was a yeti and she was – just – alive. Her long silky coat was stiff and frozen. She was deeply unconscious, but shivering so dreadfully that it seemed as though she was having convulsions; yet when they touched her forehead, it was burning hot.

"Pneumonia," said Grandma grimly.

They made themselves into a shield for her, trying to protect her from the wind, but she went on moaning and shivering. She was delirious too, thinking herself back in the valley with Lady Agatha, saying her lessons, calling to the yaks, singing the rhyming games they used to play...

"Con and Ellen have forgotten us," said Ambrose, trying to rub some warmth into his sister's hands. "They don't love us any more. They couldn't love us and leave us in this dreadful place."

And poor, simple Clarence, who so often summed up for the yetis what everyone was feeling, let a tear drop on Lucy's closed eyes and said:

"'ad. 'AD."

He meant SAD. And it was true, the yetis had never been so sad. Never in all their lives. So sad that they simply didn't want to live. Without a single shot being fired, the Hunters had already done their filthy work.

13

The Round-Up

By the second day after the yetis' kidnapping, Con and Ellen were starting to despair.

Perry, grim-faced and silent, had driven them to London. There, in his bedsit, with its portraits of famous pigs tacked on the walls, he'd developed the photos he'd taken on the journey from Nanvi Dar: photos of Uncle Otto building a campfire, of Lucy saying "sorry" to an outsize tin of baked beans, of Ambrose trying to get Hubert to sit on his knee...

With this proof that yetis really existed, they had gone into action. Perry had visited all the newspaper offices. Con and Ellen had gone with Leo Letts, the boy who was lost on the Death Peak, to the studio of the Metropolitan Television Company, which was run by his father.

"I *knew* it wasn't the dogs who found me," Leo had said, when they'd tracked him down in his smart Hampstead house. "I knew it!" And he was at once as helpful and efficient as anyone could be.

By the time the evening papers came out on that first day all of them carried pictures of the yetis, while the headlines screamed things like: ABOMINABLE

SNOWMEN COME AND GO or YETI SNATCH IN STATELY HOME or MARATHON JOURNEY ENDS IN TRAGEDY. And every hour, from the studios of the Metropolitan Television Company, there was a newsflash announcing the arrival, and kidnapping, of five Abominable Snowmen, possibly the rarest and most valuable creatures in the world.

"*Now* they'll do something, won't they?" said Con, when they came back, exhausted, to Perry's room that night. "*Now* they'll save the yetis."

But "they" didn't. Perhaps it was because no one really knew who "they" were. The police said it was nothing to do with them; they were there to catch people who had broken the law and there was no law against shooting yetis because no one had known that yetis existed. The army said it was not their business – their job was to deal with wars and revolutions and this was neither. And the Minister of the Environment didn't say anything because he was away in the Mediterranean sailing his yacht.

So on the afternoon of the second day, Con and Ellen were sitting wearily on the bed in Perry's tiny flat, while Perry made a cup of tea. All day they had been doing the rounds of government offices and departments. They had been turned away by doormen and security men. They had left messages. They had waited on uncomfortable chairs in outer offices, only to be told that unfortunately the Undersecretary for the Environment, or the Assistant Advisor to the Government Blood Sports Commission, could not see them today.

And there was only one day left. Just one short day before the hunt began.

"There has to be someone," cried Con. "Someone who has power. Someone who would *listen*."

"There is someone," said Ellen suddenly. "One person. The obvious person."

"Who?"

"The Queen. She has planes – I've heard of them. The aeroplanes of the Queen's Flight. And she is Commander-in-Chief of the armed forces. *She* could stop the Hunters."

"The Queen!" Con felt like hitting his sister because for a moment he'd really hoped. "That's rich! Two children walking into Buckingham Palace with a crazy story about yetis. Who on earth would take any notice of us?"

"No one," said Ellen. "Of us. Of two children no one would take any notice. But of two hundred – or two thousand – or twenty thousand," said Ellen, and her thin face looked as though someone had lit a lamp inside it. "We must have a demonstration, a March for the Yetis. We can demonstrate outside the palace. They'll have to listen."

"That won't be easy," said Perry, who was stirring three spoonfuls of sugar into each teacup. He knew that when you are tired and depressed sweet tea is just the thing. "I've been on one or two demos in my time, and they take weeks to organize, and you have to have permission from the police or they just come and break it up. And even so, nothing much changes."

They were quiet for a moment, sipping their scalding tea. Then Ellen said, "What else can we do?"

And as usual, she was right.

So Perry went out for fish and chips, while Con and Ellen started making posters. Con's said, ON THURSDAY THE YETIS WILL DIE ... UNLESS YOU COME, and then gave the time and place for the demonstration – Buckingham Palace, two o'clock. Ellen's said, PLEASE, PLEASE, IF YOU CARE ABOUT ANYTHING, CARE ABOUT THIS...

"Right," said Perry, when they had eaten their fish and chips and wiped the grease off their fingers. "It's just before five. I'll go and get these copied. Then you'll have to get to work."

"Aren't you coming with us?" asked Ellen.

"'fraid not," said Perry. "I've got business of my own to attend to."

Con said nothing. What could he say? Perry had brought them all the way from the Himalayas, he had helped them in a thousand ways. If he had had enough, then it was only fair; more than fair. But still, it felt like a nail in Con's heart. Now they really were on their own.

Con and Ellen didn't get back to Perry's flat until around midnight. They let themselves in with the key that Perry had given them, and sank exhausted on to the bed. They had been all over the place with their carrier bags of posters, sticking them on lamp posts and walls, in Underground train stations and bus stops. Sometimes they had been shooed away by irritated shopkeepers and traffic wardens, but sometimes they had met friendly and interested faces. An old lady with a walking stick, making her way slowly along the pavement, had asked Con what it was all about. When he explained, she said that she would tell all her friends. "Not that there are many left," she said. "And how we'll get to Buckingham Palace, I don't know." Ellen had been stopped by a bearded man who was bundled up in an old blanket in the doorway of a posh office building. Beside him sat a small dog that obviously hadn't had a bath either. The man had been mumbling quietly to himself, but when he saw Ellen he shouted suddenly, "That's it, girl, you tell those—" and he used a word that Ellen hadn't heard before, but was quite sure she shouldn't use herself.

And tomorrow was the last day. "Do you think anybody will come?" said Con. He was lying on his back in the dark, staring up at the ceiling.

"Con, I don't know, I just don't know," said Ellen. "In the morning we'll do the schools..." And then sleep took her.

For Con and Ellen, running through the London streets, jumping on to buses, fighting their way through the tunnels of the Underground, the following morning was even more exhausting than the evening before. What they had decided to do was simple enough. To call out all the schoolchildren they could find and get them to join the demonstration in front of Buckingham Palace that afternoon and beg the Queen to save the yetis.

They began in Central London, near the river and the docks, and worked their way outwards.

Sometimes they separated while Con went to a boys' school and Ellen, overcoming her shyness, tackled a girls'. Sometimes they came together again before running on to the next district and the next and the next...

The first school Con came to was called Bermeyside Primary and it was a tough one. There was a fight going on in the asphalt play yard when he arrived, and children were standing round in a circle jeering and cheering. There was no teacher to be seen. But when Con whistled, the fight broke up and the children advanced towards him. A tall boy with dreadlocks spoke.

"Yeah?"

"Listen, I need help," said Con. "Can you get this school out? The whole school? In front of Buckingham Palace at two o'clock this afternoon?"

"I can," said the boy, spitting out of the side of his mouth. "But why should I?"

Con explained about the yetis and the boy nodded. "I saw it on the telly. But man, the *Queen*. Why not the Mafia or something?"

"The Queen has her own planes. People would listen to her."

The boy stood looking down at Ambrose's photograph, which Con had brought.

"Do we get paid?"

"No. Will you come?" said Con.

He spat again. "OK," he said, holding out his hand. "I'll get them out, and I'll get my cousin Mervyn to bring out Fairfield Junior."

His next school couldn't have been more different – a little prep school inside the gates of a big house where the boys, in white flannels, were already out on the cricket field. There was the sound of clapping and polite voices saying things like: "Well played,

Johnson," and, "Good for you, Smithers!"

Con climbed over the high wall and dropped down beside a dozy-looking boy in spectacles, who was supposed to be fielding at long off but actually seemed to be searching for interesting-looking beetles.

But though he looked dozy, he was very quick on the uptake. "I saw it on TV," he said. "And I'll do everything I can to bring some people. Mind you, there are some pretty grim characters here. There's a boy called Smithers, who pops at nesting blackbirds with his air gun. But I'll do what I can. Oh, heck, there's the ball!"

And to groans and catcalls as the nice boy missed his catch, Con ran out of the high gates and on...

Ellen, meanwhile, was tackling the girls of The Sacred Heart Convent a couple of streets away. The nuns had already shooed the little girls, in their grey pleated skirts and white blouses, into the school and Ellen had to barge her way into the locker room where they were changing their outdoor shoes.

Quickly she grabbed two of them: a fat girl with freckles and a thin one with braces on her teeth, and explained what she wanted. In a minute she was surrounded by whispering, tittering children, some with one shoe on, some with none, all of them wanting to know what was happening. They sighed over Ambrose's picture, said he was just like a teddy bear, and giggled when Ellen asked them to assemble in front of Buckingham Palace. As she ran to her next school, Ellen felt thoroughly disgusted. She was sure she had wasted her time.

Yet it was those same little girls in their white blouses and knee socks who, at two o'clock that very afternoon, locked Sister Maria in the lavatory, shut the Mother Superior in the coal house and marched in an orderly crocodile to Buckingham Palace. What's more, a girl called Prudence Mallory had found time to make a banner with the words SAVE THE YETIS splashed across it in red ink. The banner was made from the calico bathrobe of Sister Theresa which another girl called Betty Bainbridge had "borrowed" when she was meant to be taking a message to Matron. All in all, Ellen had been very wrong to underrate the girls of The Sacred Heart.

Next Ellen visited a ballet school where the girls were doing pliés at the barre, and managed to get past a whistle-blowing games mistress to tackle some cold-looking high school girls stripping for gym, before she met Con again at Newlands Progressive. This was rather an alarming place: very new and fashionable with lots of glass and sculptures in the hall, and the children all seemed to come from very trendy homes. But they were certainly very quick on the uptake when it came to what they called protest. "We're not protesting," said Con, "we're asking for help."

"Of course you're protesting," said a boy of about twelve in bare feet and an Indian shirt, "you're protesting against blood sports."

Con had to agree with this. "But we want to keep it orderly."

"Oh, sure," said the boy. "Trouble with the Bill is just a waste of time."

The teacher came back then – Ellen thought him a bit shaggy for a teacher – but he listened to them, which was more than could be said for some of the others they had met. "This might be a good opportunity for a lesson in practical citizenship," he said. It was an odd place, the Newlands Progressive.

The whole morning, Con and Ellen never stopped to rest or eat as they pounded through the streets of London. They begrudged even the seconds that it took to retie their shoelaces.

Convent schools and prep schools, strict schools and sloppy schools, schools for maladjusted children and schools for little snobs... Jewish schools and French schools and Schools for the Deaf, schools run by bullies and schools run by kind and enlightened head teachers – that gruelling morning, Con and Ellen visited as many as they possibly could. But London is a big city, and there are a lot of schools. They may have broken some kind of record, but they couldn't visit them all.

And by two o'clock, half dead with fatigue, they sat on the steps of the Victoria Monument in the middle of the huge area that faces the Queen's London home. They had bought a couple of meat pies and a banana and as they munched and rubbed their aching feet, they knew they had done everything they could. There was nothing to do now except wait.

14

The Great Yeti Demonstration

"No one's going to come," said Con suddenly, in a flat, bleak voice. "We were mad to think they would. It's all been a complete failure."

"It's only half past two," said Ellen. "Remember, the schoolchildren have got to get out of their schools somehow. That isn't exactly easy. And people have jobs..."

Another five minutes, ten...

Con heard a polite cough, and turning round he saw an elderly couple smiling at him. "Have we come to the right place for the yeti demonstration?" asked the man.

"Our friend Margaret told us about it," said the woman. "She couldn't come herself; she really can't get about much. But we've brought a Thermos and a folding chair for Charles. His knees, you know."

Con said that they had come to the right place, and they set about arranging their chair and getting comfy.

Some more minutes passed.

And then, walking in a neat crocodile down the Mall, their banner torn from Sister Theresa's bathrobe waving in the breeze, came the little white-bloused girls of the Convent of The Sacred Heart. Without fuss, taking no notice of the amused stares of the passers-by and the tourists with their cameras, they bowed their heads to Con and Ellen and then went to stand in a row in front of the tall spiked railings, facing the silent sentries of the Coldstream Guards.

They had hardly got settled when, swinging across St James's Park, came a motley, long-haired crowd of boys and girls from Newlands Progressive. They had raided the art room for posters and the slogans they carried, though not always spelt quite right, were brightly painted and eye-catching. A FARE DEEL FOR YETIS, said one placard and AKTION NOW! said another. They had been singing "We Shall Overcome", accompanied by their teacher on a mandolin, as they straggled across the park, but when they reached the palace they became quiet immediately and went to stand behind the little girls of the convent, their banners pointing so that the Queen could see them.

Then a strange collection of people came shuffling across the road towards the palace. Ellen recognized the homeless man with his little dog who had shouted at her the night before. He had brought some friends with him. It was clear from their appearance that they lacked most of the necessities of life, such as hot water, beds and teeth, but they were in good spirits. Perhaps a bit too good, some of them, thought Ellen. They gathered at the railings, and struck up a conversation with the elderly couple. At first the old gentleman on his folding chair was a bit put out, but the dog soon put an end to that. He wagged his tail, politely, and Con saw the old man reach out to scratch him behind the ear. "It hasn't been the same since Buster went," he sighed. "Can't get another dog now. He'd outlive me."

And now people began to appear from everywhere. The children of Bermeyside Primary came up Buckingham Palace Road, and went to stand beside the Newlands Progressive. The boys of the cricket-playing prep school, in striped caps which made them look like little wasps, marched proudly up Constitution Hill and came to a halt behind the convent girls. Ellen's little ballet students, moving already with the grace of dancers, came in across Green Park.

And so they came. Slowly but surely the trickle became a stream, and the stream a river. There were children from schools that neither Con nor Ellen had had time to visit – and schools that Leo had called out from the north-west of London where he lived. And there were students who should have been at lectures and nannies pushing prams containing babies whose own parents were too rich to look after them. There were mothers and workmen and pensioners.

They had done it. The traffic had stopped and there were long lines of cars with puzzled people in them, hooting. Policemen appeared and looked baffled – was it some kind of rally they hadn't been told about? So many children – and where were the teachers?

"Come along, move along," they said. And people did come along and did move along, but always, quietly and obstinately, to the place they had been told to come, the great circular space outside the stately grey palace of the Queen.

There were perhaps a thousand people there by three o'clock. But an odd thing about crowds is that a thousand isn't very many. Of course in a railway station or a theatre it is a lot. But not in a huge wide concourse like the one in front of Buckingham Palace.

Con and Ellen had done their very best, no one could have done more. But you simply can't get a million people to come to a demonstration in a single day.

And now as Con climbed up the steps leading to the statue of Queen Victoria in the middle of Queen's Gardens and looked out over the crowd, he couldn't help thinking that although it was more than just a puddle of faces gazing up at him, it certainly wasn't a sea.

He raised his arms, and someone started chanting, "We want the Queen, we want the Queen!" Then others joined in, and soon they had all taken up the cry. Then Con lowered his arms, the crowd fell silent, and in his strongest voice, he spoke.

"Thank you all for coming. I shall now present our request to Her Majesty the Queen." Con was an intelligent boy and he knew that the Queen was no freer than anyone else to do what she liked, but was surrounded by officials and red tape and things that it was all right to do and things that it wasn't.

He climbed down, took the scroll of paper that Ellen handed him and began to walk towards the main entrance of the palace. By the huge gates he stopped, not quite knowing what to do. If he walked past the guards he would be challenged and turned back. Boys did not walk casually into the palace, he knew that.

While he stood there hesitating, a grey-haired man in a dark suit came out of a door further on and came towards him, past the guards. He looked pale and stern but he spoke politely to Con.

"What exactly is going on here?"

Con explained clearly and carefully about the plight of the yetis. "It's all in that bit of paper. The place they've been taken to, the latitude and longitude. The people who did it. And the time when..." – he faltered for a moment – "the time when they're going to be shot."

The man took the scroll, which had taken many hours to prepare. "I will see that it goes through the usual channels," he said.

Con didn't know what the usual channels were but he didn't like the sound of them.

"No," he said. "It's for the Queen."

"You must know," said the man impatiently, "that the Queen cannot possibly attend personally to everything that comes her way."

"Not everything," said Con. "But this."

"The Queen is not—"

"I don't know what the Queen is *not*," said Con desperately. "But what she is, surely, is someone that people can turn to when there's trouble."

"I have no further comment," sniffed the man. "You must disperse this crowd immediately, or I shall be obliged to have you arrested for unlawful assembly, disturbing the peace and," he added, as the little dog lifted his leg against one of the stone gateposts, "fouling royal property." Then he turned away and went back into the palace.

"We're staying till something is done," shouted Con to his departing back. But the man showed no sign of having heard.

Half an hour, an hour, and still the crowd stood there, their faces lifted to the great façade of the palace. Newlands Progressive struck up a rousing chorus of "We shall not, we shall not be moved". And then a wave of whispering passed through them.

"Did you see her?"

"It was her, I'm sure."

"A face. There by the window."

"It's the Queen. She's going to come out, I know she is."

But the woman whose face they had glimpsed at the huge first-floor window did not come out on to the balcony.

"She's gone."

"She's not coming!"

"It wasn't her. It was the housekeeper."

"Or a lady-in-waiting."

Suddenly, disappointment swept the crowd. They realized how tired they were, how hungry.

For Con it was worse. It wasn't going to work. The great yeti demonstration was over, and just as Perry had warned, nothing had changed. All this time he had been telling himself that if he worked hard enough, cared enough, he could save the day like some hero in a story. For him it wasn't only about saving a threatened species, about stopping blood sports and meaningless killing. For Con, to fail was to fail his friends; to fail Lucy, Uncle Otto, Clarence, Grandma and Ambrose. They were innocent, and kind, and they had trusted him. He had brought them halfway across the world to certain death. It was unbearable.

Con felt rage rising inside him. He thought he would choke. He ran to the statue, clambered up, and began to shout.

"We've failed. It's useless. Go home. Nobody listens to children and tramps and old ladies, and nobody ever will. Go home. You've heard all that stuff – 'Might is right', 'Money talks'. Well it's true. It's all true. The killing and the hating will never stop. If you say you don't like it, they'll call you a wimp or a wet or a dreamer. If you say there is another, kinder, more thoughtful way, they'll call you a lunatic. If you go on saying it, they'll probably shoot you. Go home." Con paused for breath. Ellen was crying and telling him to stop, but he was just getting warmed up. He had plenty more to say. "And as for the Queen," shouted Con, but nobody ever knew what he was going to say about her, because his voice was drowned by the rumbling growl of a big diesel engine being revved – an engine with a dodgy, clattering water pump. All heads turned, and sure enough, straight up the wide Mall towards Buckingham Palace came a canary yellow articulated

lorry with COLD CARCASSES in large letters on its side. After it, in a long line, came more lorries. There was a low-loader, a giant removal van, a huge-wheeled quarry truck, a spanking new Scania heavy haulage vehicle lit up like a Christmas tree.

The yellow lorry drove up to the palace, and as the crowd parted and cheered wildly, it parked right across the front of the main gates, blocking them completely.

Perry jumped out the cab, looking pleased with himself.

"Oh, Perry, you came back!" Ellen rushed over to him and hugged him. "But it's no good, they're going to arrest us."

"Are they now?" said Perry. "Just give me a few moments to get my mates organized, and we'll have a little chat."

Quickly, he directed the massive vehicles to park across every entrance to the palace. The three big gates at the front were blocked. The other lorries drove round and out of sight, to block the rear entrances.

"Right," said Perry. "That should do it. She won't be taking delivery of any groceries for a while."

When they were ensconced in the familiar cab and Perry was enjoying a well-earned cuppa, Con said, "You're going to get into awful trouble. You can't just lock the Queen into her own palace."

"I haven't locked her in," said Perry, "I've locked everybody else out. It's a picket. Legitimate industrial action. I had a word with some mates about it, and we agreed it was worth a try. I'm not saying it'll work, mind you," he said, directing his words to Con, "but I've learned one thing after all the scrapes I've been in, and that is never give up. And trust your friends," he added.

Ellen blushed. "We thought you'd just gone away..."

"What happens now?" said Con hastily.

"Now," said Perry, "we wait."

They didn't have to wait long. The police hadn't been particularly worried by a peaceful demonstration of children and unimportant people outside Buckingham Palace, but now the wail of sirens was heard and flashing blue lights converged on the scene from all directions. A whole fleet of police cars drew up, and uniformed men started pouring out of them. Perry and the other drivers had formed a line in front of Perry's lorry, with arms folded. They weren't all big and beefy, though the man from the removal van looked pretty fearsome, but they didn't look as though they were going to budge in the face of the massed officers of the law. The policemen stopped at a safe distance from the drivers, and the man in charge produced a loudhailer. His voice echoed over the heads of the crowd.

"You are breaking the law. You must cease this action immediately and remove your vehicles."

Perry didn't need a loudhailer.

"Remove them yourself," he roared back, "if you can." And he held up a handful of wiring. All the drivers had disabled their engines, and it would take many hours to make them work again. They had a good laugh at that.

"You are all under arrest," came the voice from the loudhailer, "and we are now obliged to take you into custody."

The policemen took out their batons and began to walk forward. A couple of the drivers clenched their fists, and the driver of the removal van produced a mole wrench from his overalls. It was going to get ugly. The remaining demonstrators started booing the police, and chanting "Save the yetis".

Then something made the advancing police stop. A big black car rounded the monument and drove towards the blockading lorries, right between the line of men in their blue uniforms, and the grim-faced drivers. There was a little flag on the bonnet of the car. A young fit-looking man jumped out of the front passenger seat, and ran round the car to open one of the rear doors. Out stepped a tall, well-dressed man with thinning hair and a face which reminded one of a rather sad sheep. Ellen, who had been watching everything from the cab of Perry's lorry, thought she had seen him before somewhere. He walked towards Perry, and stopped in front of him.

"Excuse me," he said, "but one would rather like to drive in and have one's dinner."

Ellen had never seen Perry flustered before, but she saw it now. He actually stammered. "W-well, sir … I'm afraid you can't. The yetis are going to die if we don't stop it somehow."

"Ah yes, the yetis, I read about that, a nasty business."

There was a silence, which seemed to go on for a very long time.

"Coldwater Straits, is that right?"

"Yes, sir."

"Ah, jolly good. That's in BAT, I believe. Now if I can just squeeze past, then perhaps I could have a word with Mother."

Perry stepped aside, and the tall man pressed himself through the narrow gap between the lorry and the railings, and disappeared into the palace.

Everything went very quiet. The police didn't move, the drivers didn't move.

"In bat? Cricketer, is he?" growled the removal van man.

"Why did you let him through?" called Con. "You said it was a picket."

"That bloke," said Perry, "is the only hope we have left."

Time passed very slowly. The few demonstrators

that remained gathered in small groups and talked quietly among themselves. Some reporters arrived, and a van from one of the television networks.

Somewhere in the palace, in a comfortable sitting room with thick carpets and a fire burning in the grate, a delicate hand put down the teacup it had been holding, and reached for the telephone.

For the rest of their lives, there was one moment that Con and Ellen always remembered. As the evening settled down and became night, and all over London the street lights blinked into life, the people outside the palace waited: Perry and the drivers, the remaining demonstrators, quite a lot of them schoolchildren who knew that their parents would be worried sick, the policemen. Only the uniformed driver of the big black car didn't wait. He drove off to put his car in the garage and have his supper.

And then, from one of the doors in the façade of the palace, the grey-haired official emerged and crossed the wide front terrace towards them. They watched him in utter silence as he approached the railings and stopped. He reached into the inside pocket of his suit and brought out an embossed envelope. He poked it rather unceremoniously through the railings into Con's hand, turned on his heel, and departed.

Con saw the royal seal, a magnificent coat of arms with a lion and a unicorn on it. He handed it to Perry.

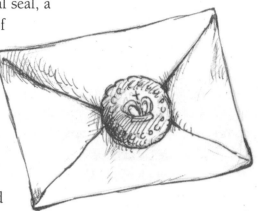

"You read it, Perry. I daren't."

Perry read it, and in a strange choked voice as though he was getting a cold he said, "All right, Con, up you go. They have a right to hear this.".

He gave Con a leg up on to the top of the cab and, from there, Con scrambled on to the roof of the lorry. He didn't need to shout this time for every face was turned towards him, and the only sound was the ever-present thrum of the big city.

"We have an answer," he cried. "I shall read it to you:

"*We have this day in accordance with the petition of our subjects instructed George Ullaby RN, commander of Her Majesty's Research Vessel* Seadog, *stationed in* the Weddell Sea, to proceed with all possible speed to Coldwater Straits and in liaison with the staff of the British Antarctic Territory Research Station, there to prevent by any legitimate means at their disposal the unlawful, cruel and inhumane destruction of the yetis.

"'We thereby require and request, in recognition of the granting of this petition and in anticipation of the successful outcome of this mission, that the vehicles at present obstructing the entrances to our Royal Residence might be removed with dispatch, because the bin-men come on Fridays.'

"We did it," said Con. "Thank you, oh thank you all so very much."

And he started to cry.

It was quite a party. The police gave up any attempt to be proper police. There was so much hugging and backslapping going on, that they really couldn't call it an unlawful assembly. You can't arrest people for laughing and dancing – well, not in England you can't. Some of the constables got straight to work helping the drivers to fix their lorries, sharing jokes about what they had seen on the roads of Great Britain – lorry drivers and policemen are out in all weathers. The Newlands teacher, who had become a royalist, borrowed the loudhailer and started to sing

"God Save The Queen". The old gentleman offered the homeless man a drink from his Thermos, which turned out to contain a pretty decent Speyside malt whisky, and before you could say knife they had decided to set up a kennel in the country to breed Jack Russells, which after a long argument was the only breed they could both agree was a really nice little dog.

There were some unfortunate moments – there always are at a real shindig. Some of the Newland Progressive pupils went skinny-dipping in the Serpentine, and persuaded three girls from the convent school to come along. A small boy from the prep school was violently sick after winning a packet of cigarettes off one of the Bermeyside kids in a hastily assembled game of Texas Hold 'em poker on the flatbed of the low-loader. Still, a party is a party. What can you do?

But before long the celebrations came to an end, and Con and Ellen were on their way home to Perry's little flat, hardly able to keep their eyes open, and still unable to believe that there was real hope for their threatened friends far away on the treacherous ice.

15

The Attack

On the terrible, bleak ice of the Antarctic, the yetis had given up all hope. It was their third night on the ice without food and shelter and it didn't seem possible that Lucy could live through another one. She was quite unconscious; her breath came in shallow, rasping pants and even in that terrible cold she burned with fever. Grandma's teeth were chattering so much that Uncle Otto had had to jam a piece of ice between them to stop her jaw from breaking. Clarence lay beside Lucy, despairing and as still as a stone. Only Ambrose, who had loved people so much, still believed that somehow they would be rescued.

"When an aeroplane comes we must run and shout and wave our arms," he said for the hundredth time.

None of the others answered. They couldn't hear him. Their ear lids had been iced to their ears. The yetis had cried easily but now there were no tears frozen to their furry cheeks. The despair they felt was far too great for tears. And at last Ambrose, too, lay down and waited for the end.

It was their iced-up ear lids that stopped them,

at first, from hearing the drone of engines coming towards them. Five engines. Five snowmobiles: huge, armoured monsters, part tank, part sledge, purpose-built for the hunt, pushing steadily onwards through the desert of snow and ice.

In the first of the snowmobiles sat Colonel Bagwackerly, the president of the Hunter's Club, and the MacDermot-Duff. Their eyes shone with greed and excitement, their automatic rifles were loaded and ready, and on the floor beside them was a sack. Not an ordinary sack. An outsize one, especially made so that it could take the dead body of a yeti.

There were five such sacks, one for each yeti, one in each snowmobile.

"You don't think that mealy little worm Prink'll blow the gaff, do you?" said the MacDermot-Duff. He had stuffed his kilt and sporran inside a quilted flying suit and looked like a large and lumpy liver sausage. "We ought really to have shot him."

"Dash it, man, he is human," said Bagwackerly, flicking the ice crystals from his sticky moustache. And when his companion looked a bit doubtful he added, "Anyway, I was at school with his cousin."

They pressed on, their specially built snowmobiles negotiating the broken surface and ridges of ice with ease. This was going to be the hunt to end all hunts! There weren't going to be many clubs in the world with five stuffed yetis on their walls – perhaps the only yetis in the world! Why one skin alone would be worth a king's ransom!

"Spilt blood is glorious, killing is grand, hunters victorious conquer the land," sang Bagwackerly above the noise of the engine. It was the club song and a perfectly disgusting one, but then the Hunters were disgusting people.

Behind them, in the second snowmobile, was the Sheik of Dabubad with some of his friends. The sheik had murdered all the swift cheetahs and tawny lions and fleet-footed gazelles in the golden plains around his palace and now thirsted for a new kind of slaughter. Behind him came Herr Blutenstein, gibbering with excitement. This was better than schtick-pigging!

"There!" said Bagwackerly suddenly. "Do you see?"

He pointed forward to where some dark shapes could just be made out against the featureless ice.

"It's them all right!" said the MacDermot-Duff, his black eyes popping with excitement.

"Get out the guns," ordered Bagwackerly. And the snowmobiles came steadily on...

"Oh, look! People are coming! In those funny black things. It's Con and Ellen! We're going to be rescued," cried Ambrose the Abominable, leaping to his feet.

The others lifted their weary faces. Making a great effort, they forced their ear lids open. Then, stiffly, without hope at first, they raised their shaggy arms and waved.

"Ambrose is right. It is help after all," said Uncle Otto unbelievingly.

"God has heard us," said Grandma. "It's me singing all those hymns."

Lucy was too weak to move, but for the first time since her illness she opened her eyes and a shy and hopeful smile appeared on her gentle face.

"They've got some sort of stick things in their hands," said Ambrose. "I expect it's bamboo shoots because they're our favourites."

And then it happened. Spattering the ice, the bullets bounced and ricocheted, a hail of death.

"Bullets! " said Grandma unbelievingly. "They're shooting from those sledge things."

The snowmobiles came closer. There was another burst of fire.

"But there's nothing to shoot at here," said Ambrose, peering at the empty, desolate waste.

"Yes, there is," said Uncle Otto, and he spoke in a voice they had never heard him use before. "There is something to shoot at here. Us."

"Damn it, missed," cursed Colonel Bagwackerly. "It's this darned machine jigging about. Can't you hold it steady?"

"I am holding it steady," snapped the MacDermot-Duff.

"Well, I'm not letting those cross-eyed wallies behind us get in first. They're blasted foreigners and I'm the club President. We've got to move in closer."

So the MacDermot-Duff jammed his feet down on

the accelerator and the armoured sledge lurched forward.

"There! Winged one!" shrieked Bagwackerly. "Look, he's fallen, the hairy brute. It's a big one, too! We've done it! The first yeti ever, and I, Cyril Bagwackerly, shot it!"

"It's nothing..." said Uncle Otto, as Grandma and Ambrose ran up to him. "Just ... my leg."

But the wound was a bad one. Blood poured in jagged spurts through the thick fur. An artery had been hit.

Desperately, the others tried to stop the bleeding, closing the wound with their fingers, laying their cheeks against it, but they had nothing. No cloth to make a tourniquet, no bandage.

"They're closing in," said Grandma. "It won't be long now. At least we can die like Christians. Say your prayers, Ambrose, like Lady Agatha would want you to."

But Ambrose was beyond saying anything. If people could do that – if they could come across the ice and shoot kind, good Uncle Otto – then let death come, and come quickly. Ambrose the Abominable was through.

But the men in the snowmobiles did not come on. Their machines had stopped, their greedy, glittering eyes were turned in amazement to the sky.

Aeroplanes. The sky had suddenly filled with planes, skimming low towards them across the ice.

"What the devil?" said Bagwackerly. "Those aren't ours."

"If anyone's trying to get in ahead of us and bag themselves a yeti there's going to be trouble," snarled the MacDermot-Duff. "Those hairy brutes are ours, every one of them."

All the Hunters were sitting back now, looking up through their snow goggles at the sky.

"Schweinehunde!" yelled Herr Blutenstein, shaking his fists. "You schall not schteel my yeti schkinn!"

"Pariah dogs," screamed the Sheik. "Poachers! I'll have you whipped!"

"Quickly, reload, everybody," shouted Bagwackerly, gesturing to make himself heard above the roaring of the planes. "Move in for the kill. We'll get in first. We'll show 'em!"

And in all the snowmobiles, the Hunters, terrified of being done out of their spoils, reloaded their guns and started their machines.

"Ready!" screeched Bagwackerly, and the Hunters gunned their engines and set off at full throttle to finish the job.

But up above them, others were ready too. The aircraft, after circling once, now lined themselves up and flew in low over the snowmobiles. The fuselage doors opened and five long black muzzles emerged.

The Hunters did not have time to scream "Cannons!" or even to notice that it was not the yetis that were being attacked but they themselves before it happened.

"Uuugwaa! Blubble-hoo!" gurgled Bagwackerly. "I'm drowning. I'm choking! Uroo!"

"It's poison, it's ... aauuua gug... I can't see. I can't move! Yak glumph," spluttered the MacDermot-Duff.

"Hilfe! Hulp! I schtuck am," yelled Herr Blutenstein. "I am schtuck." He was indeed stuck. His behind was stuck to his seat, his gloved hands were stuck to his gun, his gun was stuck to his snowmobile, and his nostrils and eyelids were stuck together.

The other Hunters were stuck as well. However, the McDermott-Duff came unstuck again fairly quickly. His hands had stuck to the throttle of his machine, and it careered off at full speed straight into a big frozen ice block. With a cracking sound, the McDermott-Duff was wrenched free and flew like a guided missile before landing with a strange tinkling sound and spinning over the ice for about a hundred metres.

Bagwackerly had been leaning out of the snowmobile to get a clear shot at the yetis, and so much of him was stuck to various parts of the vehicle that even a head-on collision couldn't budge him. The shock of the crash was pretty devastating, however, because it dislodged his nose from the barrel of his gun. Well, most of his nose (it was a long one). The rest of it remained attached to his rifle.

All the other snowmobiles came quickly to a halt as their engines spluttered and died. They had been black and fierce-looking machines, but now they were white and glittery like Christmas decorations. Inside them, the men mumbled and struggled for a while, and then stopped moving entirely. In one of them, the Sheikh of Dabubad was standing like a statue. He was childish and badly brought up, and at the moment of the attack he had been sticking his tongue out at the approaching planes. Now he couldn't get it back in, because it was connected to his right foot by a long column of glittering ice.

The men and women of the British Antarctic Survey had been instructed not to kill and they hadn't killed. But it seemed a pity to waste the latest tear gas or rubber bullets on men as vile and foolish as the Hunters. So they had decided on something much cheaper, simpler, and, in the Antarctic, effective. Water. They were intelligent young people, who knew that the speed of the snowmobiles would make the frozen air even colder, and that water would freeze in seconds. So they had simply pumped a few hundred gallons of water from high-pressure hoses, and encased everything in ice.

The young research assistant who jumped from the cockpit of the Twin Otter as it skidded to a halt on the pack ice found the yetis as still as statues, waiting for death. He walked across the rough ice towards them, his pack of emergency supplies on his back and then, as he saw the blood staining the ice, he started to run.

"It's all right," he shouted. "The Hunters are being rounded up and we have come to take you away."

When he saw Uncle Otto's wound he was white with fury. "Inhuman abominable monsters," he muttered, and he certainly didn't mean the yetis. He bent down and began to unwrap the disinfectant and bandages from the pack he carried.

"I ... expect ... it was an accident," said Uncle Otto, good and noble yeti that he was.

But Ambrose, who had been so loving and trusting all his life, stared at the young man with his wall eyes and said: "It wasn't an accident. They did it on purpose. People are bad."

16

Ambrose Gives Up

The hospital they brought the yetis to was a very famous one in a quiet London square. The nurses were kind and skilful, the doctors clever and comforting and the matron wasn't the starched and stuffy kind but a sympathetic person who let Con and Ellen stay with the yetis all day long, because she knew that people can't get well if they are separated from those they love.

The yetis had become very famous after the children's protest outside the palace and the rescue by the seaplanes of the British Antarctic Territory Research Station, and the nurses were kept busy shooing journalists and cameramen out of the wards. Perry had gone down to Somerset to look for his pig farm, but Con and Ellen had to have a police escort when they went to and from the hospital because of the newspapermen dogging them. And every night on television there was a bulletin about the yetis, and when it was on the streets emptied, as bicycles and footballs were abandoned and children all over the country went inside to watch the news.

At first the news was grave. Lucy was very ill with

pneumonia and Uncle Otto's wound was so deep that he had to have a long and difficult operation to remove the bullet. Both his and Lucy's bed had the curtains drawn round them while doctors and nurses hurried backwards and forwards with syringes and trays of medicine and thermometers.

But slowly they both got better. They could tell that Lucy had turned the corner when she asked the nurses for a mirror and started worrying about the state of her stomach. "It's my pigtails," she murmured groggily. "They're all undone."

So the nurses, neat as only nurses can be, made her two lovely plaits all ready for Queen Victoria if they found her again. After that Lucy managed to say "Sorry" to a plate of soup which the ward maid brought her. The next morning she said "Sorry" to three boiled eggs, some grilled tomatoes and the bunch of marigolds in a vase beside her bed. After that she was reckoned to be out of danger.

Uncle Otto's wound, too, healed well. Soon he was walking on crutches, looking somehow very manly and distinguished as people on crutches are apt to do, and it was now that something very nice happened to him. The clever doctors had found something to rub into his bald patch which *wasn't* toothpaste or honey or cream cheese but a real medicine which someone had just invented to make hair grow. And almost day by day, as he lay in bed reading the books the kind library lady had brought him on a trolley, they could see the soft, dark down which covered his domed head grow steadily longer and stronger.

Grandma, of course, loved being in hospital. Being old, she had quite a lot of interesting things wrong with her like heartburn and fibroids and wind, which everybody in the hospital took seriously instead of just saying, "We must expect a few troubles as we get older," like Lady Agatha had done.

A lot of doctors came to see Clarence too, and put electrodes on his brain and tried to make him read things. But when the others explained that Clarence's brain had been damaged when he was little and that he was very happy as he was and that they all loved him, they very sensibly left him alone.

With everything going so well, with messages coming in that the Hunters had been turned out of Farley Towers and the proper owner was coming back, with Mr Bellamy phoning to say that the children could stay as long as necessary, Con and Ellen should have been as happy as could be. In fact, they were worried sick.

And what they were worried about was Ambrose.

In the hospital, when the yetis first came, they hadn't taken too much notice of Ambrose. He didn't have pneumonia like Lucy, or a gaping wound like Uncle Otto. He wasn't old like Grandma and bits of his brain weren't missing like Clarence's. A bit of rest and warmth, thought the staff, and Ambrose, who was young and strong, would soon be himself again.

But Ambrose didn't get well and strong, and Ambrose wasn't himself again. When Con pointed out to the nurses that he wasn't eating – wasn't eating at *all* – they told him not to worry. "Young people often go off their food, especially after a shock. Just take no notice."

So the children tried not to make a fuss as Ambrose sent away trayfuls of egg and chips, of castle puddings and banana custard. They tried not to worry when Ambrose lay there with his blue eye dull and sunken and his brown eye glazed and staring at the ceiling. They tried not to worry when Ambrose wouldn't even look up at the telly, though they were showing a Tom and Jerry cartoon.

"Shall I tell you a story, Ambrose?" Con begged.

But Ambrose just shook his great, shaggy head and sighed.

From the first moment she had found him, wall-eyed and crumpled and desperate to be loved, Lady Agatha had known that Ambrose wasn't quite like the others. "I really think you could *kill* Ambrose by thinking unkind thoughts about him," she had said to Con in the valley of Nanvi Dar. Since then, Ambrose had seen people come over the ice with guns; he had seen his uncle shot; he had known hatred.

And now he turned his face to the wall and prepared to die.

In a week or so the doctors and nurses became worried too. There was talk of force-feeding and intravenous drips and things which made the children's blood run cold when they heard of them. And on the news bulletins, now, it was announced that though the other four yetis were improving steadily, there was slight concern about the youngest, Ambrose the Abominable.

After a few more days the "slight concern" was changed to "serious concern".

At night, the doctors made Ellen sleep in a spare room, she was so exhausted from the strain. But nothing could shift Con. He sat by Ambrose's bed murmuring to him, telling him jokes, begging him for Lady Agatha's sake, for Father's sake, to make an effort – to eat something, to get well. But Ambrose just said, "People are *not* my brothers," and grew steadily weaker and more lifeless and ill. Until a day came when the television newscaster looked out of the screen in a very serious way and said: "It is feared that there is little hope for the youngest of the yetis, Ambrose the Abominable, now seriously ill at Park Square Hospital, London."

In the silent hospital, Con sat by Ambrose's bed, trying to believe the unbelievable. There was no hope. It was going to happen. Ambrose the Abominable was going to die.

All day, children had thronged the square outside and stood silently, their faces turned to the hospital windows, waiting for news. Now it was night. Out in the corridor the sister on duty sat in her glass cubicle guarding the white and disinfected room where Ambrose lay.

Inside the room there was no sound – even the soughing of the ventilator had ceased. Ambrose's eyes were closed, his breath would not have stirred a feather. It could not be long now.

Suddenly in the corridor outside there was a scuffle. Then a voice: high and sharp and bossy, saying, "Let me go! Let me go at once!"

The door opened and a girl came into the room. She was about Con's own age, with long, fair hair and grey eyes. She was wearing faded jeans and an old sweater and a haversack hung over one shoulder.

"Is that Ambrose?" she said, still in that loud, high voice, pointing to the bed.

Con nodded, frowning at her to be quiet. Where on earth had he heard a voice like that? And why was her face so familiar?

"Who are you?" he said.

"I'm Aggie. I came as soon as I heard. They'd walled me up in some beastly boarding school in Switzerland and I had to get back."

She went over to the bed and stood looking down at Ambrose.

"He's bad, isn't he?"

"Yes." Con had stopped trying to think where he could have seen the girl before. What did it matter? What did anything matter?

Aggie put down her haversack. Then she bent over Ambrose and still in that high, clear, governessy voice said: "And what, pray, do you think you are doing?"

Con glared at her. No one had spoken above a whisper in that room for days. Yet something held him back from interfering.

"Open your eyes at once!" the bossy voice went on. "*And* your ear lids. You're supposed to have been brought up as a Farlingham. Let's see you behave like one."

To Con's amazement, a flicker passed over Ambrose's face. A chink of blue appeared, then a chink of brown. The left ear lid wavered...

"That's better. And what does one do when a lady comes into the room?"

"Stand ... up," came a thread of a voice from the bed.

"Quite right. So you can *sit* up for a start."

And, unbelievably, Ambrose really did begin to move up on the pillow, almost to raise his head.

"I suppose you realize that dying is Very Bad Manners," the relentless girl went on.

"Is ... it?"

"Certainly it is. What are manners *for*?"

"Making ... people ... comfortable," Ambrose managed to bring out.

"Exactly. Well who's going to be comfortable if you die?" said Aggie briskly. "Sad, that's what they're going to be. What's that by your bed?"

"It's ... my ... milk."

"Your milk! Standing there gathering dust! I'm surprised at you, Ambrose. Drink it up at once," said Aggie, sounding more than ever like an old-fashioned governess.

"I ... can't."

"*Can't*, Ambrose? Or do you mean *won't*?"

She took the glass and put it in Ambrose's hands. Then she raised his head from the pillow and put her own hand under it for support. And Con, who had understood at last what it was all about, looked on, blinking back tears, while Ambrose said weakly, "Yes, Lady Agatha. I'm sorry, Lady Agatha," and drank his milk. Every single drop.

17

Home

As soon as it was clear that Ambrose was going to get quite well again, Aggie went down to Farley Towers to get it ready for the yetis.

Farley Towers belonged to her. Her real name was Lady Agatha Caroline Emma Hope Farlingham and since her father had died in a sailing accident and her mother had married again, Aggie had inherited it. But when Con tried to explain to Ambrose that Aggie was Lady Agatha's great-great-niece, Ambrose just shook his head. "No, she's our own Lady Agatha come back again," he said. "You see, Lady Agatha was awfully tired of her old body, she told us, so she just died and went up to heaven quickly and came down again in a nice new one."

And the other yetis, looking very splendid in their hospital dressing gowns, nodded their heads and said, "You can *see* she's our own Lady Agatha; you can see."

So Con, who knew that people think differently about dying in the place the yetis came from, didn't try to argue any more.

It was a golden day in late summer when the hospital ambulances, with a special police escort, brought the yetis, with Con and Ellen, to Farley Towers. Aggie was waiting on the steps to greet them and beside her, getting his front feet tangled in the shoe scraper and bleating like a foghorn, stood Hubert.

The yetis were so happy to see them both that they ran into the house without thinking. But inside the hall they hesitated.

Suppose the THINGS were still on the walls?

But of course they weren't. Aggie had been in such a temper when she saw them that she and her nice old butler had worked from dawn to dusk, stripping the walls and throwing all the stuffed heads and mounted tusks and stretched skins into the lake.

And now Farley Towers was just as Lady Agatha had described it to the yetis in the valley of Nanvi Dar. There were patchwork covers on the four-poster beds, the smell of wax polish on the cedar-wood floors, and bowls of roses on the gate-legged tables. But instead of one sacred relic under a glass case there were now two, because Aggie had found Ambrose's bedsock and washed it and put it with the other one.

Soon the yetis were settled in so happily at Farley

Towers that it was hard to believe that they had not spent all their lives in an English stately home. Grandma took over the housework, vanishing with the Hoover and a packet of sandwiches in the morning, and the sound of her singing "Oh, Happy Band of Pilgrims" would grow fainter and fainter as she hoovered herself away through the Gold drawing room and the Blue salon, reappearing in the evening through the armoury, the banqueting hall and the Spanish dining room.

Lucy tended the flower gardens, and after Aggie had told her which flowers were which, Lucy was most helpful, saying, "Sorry, thistle; sorry, dandelion; sorry, goosegrass," but never – well, hardly ever – saying, "Sorry, dahlia," or "Sorry, lily," or "Sorry, delphinium," so that soon the flower borders looked almost as tidy as in the old days when there had been no less than five gardeners at Farley.

Clarence made himself useful on the farm. All animals like yetis, but simple-minded yetis they really love, and Clarence only had to look at the chickens and they would start laying eggs. As for Uncle Otto, he shut himself into the library and started putting things to rights. The books at Farley had been allowed to get into an awful muddle: Astrology next to Zoology, Mineralogy muddled up with Entomology and Geology absolutely all over the place. Sorting all that out was going to  keep Uncle Otto busy and happy for years.

But it was Ambrose who really saved the fortunes of Farley Towers and he did this by being open to the public. All the yetis had become very famous: people wrote books about them, there was a story about them on the telly and the Queen still sent them hampers of good things from her country homes. But because he had so nearly died, or perhaps because he was the youngest, and wall-eyed into the bargain, Ambrose was, perhaps, the most famous yeti of them all.

And when they realized that it was not having any

money that forced Aggie's trustees to rent her house to the beastly Hunters, they had had the brilliant idea of opening the house to the public once a week and letting Ambrose receive the visitors.

So every Saturday the gates of Farley were thrown open and people came in cars, or on foot, or in charabancs, and paid their money to look round the house where the yetis lived and shake Ambrose by the hand and get his autograph. And when Uncle Otto and Con, who were the best at sums, added up the money at the end of the day, they found that even when they'd paid for food and fuel there was still something left over to make Farley lovelier, like putting new windows in the orangery or buying some peacocks for the terrace.

There was only one person at Farley who did not seem to be completely happy and that was Hubert. Mothers were tame stuff to Hubert now – he had grown out of them. As for fathers, how could he ever hope to find one to compare with El Magnifico? As he dug Hubert Holes all over Farley's velvet lawns, Hubert sometimes had the look of a yak who wonders what life is *for*. And then, not long before Con and Ellen were due to fly back to their father in Bukhim, something happened to change all that.

They were having elevenses on the terrace when a red delivery van swept up the drive and drew to a halt on the gravel. Then two men got out and set a big crate down on the ground.

"'esent!" said Clarence excitedly as they all clustered round. "'esent. 'esent!"

And it *was* a present. Shaken out of its layers of straw it turned out to be – an animal. But an animal unlike anything they'd ever seen.

Its back end was pink and plump and had a corkscrew tail. Its front end was white with black spots, and droopy ears that brushed the ground. In the middle, where the two ends joined, was a curvy, buff-coloured stomach and a forest of tufty hairs.

It was Con who guessed. "It's the Perrington Porker!" he cried. "Perry's done it! It's the Perrington Porker without a doubt."

And of course it was.

The yetis were enchanted. "It's a *lovely* pet for us," said Ambrose, his blue eye shining.

"Let's call him Alfred. A nice, sensible name is Alfred," said Grandma.

But the little pig didn't seem to care *what* he was called. He had eyes for only one person. The yak, Hubert.

Leaving skid marks on the gravel in his eagerness,

the porker slithered to Hubert's side. Then, squealing with pleasure, he began to butt the dishevelled yak in his tattered stomach, to nuzzle him with his pink Hoover of a nose, to stand up on his flea-sized trotters and try to climb up Hubert's tail...

For a moment, Hubert seemed to be completely stunned. Then suddenly it hit him. And as he began to lick the little pig, he seemed to grow taller, his boot face took on a look of dignity and pride, his knock knees straightened.

This was the real thing. Not *looking* for a father. *Being* one!

A week later, a Queen's Messenger arrived at Farley in a black Rolls-Royce to arrange for Con and Ellen's journey back to Nanvi Dar. It was the tired man in the dark suit who had taken Con's petition into the palace, and it was from him they learnt that Parliament had passed a law turning yetis into Very Important Creatures or VICs and that harming them was now a crime which carried the worst punishment in the land.

As for the Hunters, they were still in prison. The police had been forced to let them go at first, because at the time of the kidnapping there had been no law against shooting yetis, because no one knew that yetis existed. But when the Hunters had been freed for a few days they came and hammered on the prison gates and asked to be taken back inside. This was because the people of Britain were so angry at what they had done to the yetis that boys threw stones at them, and old ladies bonked them on the head with shopping baskets, and men coming out of pubs threatened to beat them up.

Mr Prink, however, wasn't in prison. Often he wished he was, because he was somewhere even worse – back with Mrs Prink, who made him gargle with carbolic soap and clean out the budgerigar and eat up the gristle in his mutton fat.

And now the dreaded day came when Con and Ellen were due to leave Farley Towers. They had put it off as long as possible, but though Mr Bellamy had written brave and cheerful letters he had not been able to hide how much he missed them.

Although the helicopter which was to take them to the airport was not expected till midday, the yetis had already put in several hours' hard crying time by breakfast.

"It's not good for people to lose their friends," wailed Ambrose. "It makes them all lumpy in the stomach."

"We'll be back, Ambrose," said Ellen. "You know we will." But she soaked three whole handkerchiefs herself before the drone of the helicopter was heard above the roofs of Farley.

The helicopter landed neatly on the lawns. The pilot opened the door of the cockpit and jumped out. Then he walked round to open the other door. And the yetis stared in disbelief as a tall, strong, marvellously furry figure stepped majestically down on to the grass.

"Father!" they cried, surging forward. "It's Father come back to us! It's our very own Father."

The joy of having him back was so great that they could hardly speak. Uncle Otto had been marvellous but Father – well, Father was Father and they knew now that they need never be afraid again.

Father's first words, however, were grave and sad.

"From the fact that I am here," he said solemnly, "you will know that our beloved Lady Agatha has died. Her end was peaceful and she lies where she wished to lie in the cool earth of our—"

"No, she doesn't," squeaked Ambrose, while Father frowned at him reprovingly. "She doesn't lie, she..."

But Father had stopped taking any notice of Ambrose. He was staring at the steps of the terrace which led down to the lawn.

Aggie had been inside the house when the

helicopter arrived, preparing the yetis' lunch. Now she came down the steps slowly, carrying a tray of drinks. Her long, white cooking apron came to her ankles, her fair hair blew in the breeze, her grey eyes were intent on the brimming mugs.

Father had taken a few steps forward and then stopped. There was amazement in his wise old eyes, and a deep and shining joy.

"That's how she looked when I carried her away from her tent," he said. "Exactly like that!"

Almost unbearably moved, the dignified old yeti walked over to Aggie.

"You've come back to us, Lady Agatha," he said, and bent his head and took the tray from her hands.

And Con and Ellen saw that the story which had begun a hundred years ago in the mountains of Tibet had ended, and that their work was done, and they got into the helicopter and flew away.

About the Illustrator

SHARON RENTTA has always had a passion for drawing and knew from a young age that she wanted to pursue a career in illustration. She grew up in Chester, where she completed a year's foundation course before doing a BA (Hons) in Graphic Design at the Liverpool John Moore's University. Afterwards she graduated from the prestigious Cambridge School of Art with an MA in Children's Book Illustration. Since then, Sharon has written and illustrated six full-colour picture books, and her black-and-white line illustrations in Eva Ibbotson's ONE DOG AND HIS BOY have attracted widespread acclaim.

Sharon lives in Cambridge with her husband and works in her studio at home. When she is not drawing and painting and making stories, she enjoys reading, pottering about in the garden, an occasional jog and always a good action movie.

Books by Sharon Rentta

Sidney the Little Blue Elephant
Sidney Goes to School
Dogs Go Shopping
A Day with the Animal Doctors
A Day with the Animal Firefighters
A Day with the Animal Builders (coming in 2013)

sharon-rentta.co.uk

Sharon says of illustrating THE ABOMINABLES:

"*I was so delighted when I found out that another novel by Eva Ibbotson had been discovered, and even more excited to be asked to illustrate it. When I started to read it, I just couldn't put it down! I was so captivated by these strange yetis, with their back-to-front feet, whose characters were described and developed with such warmth and humour.*

It was a happy, if somewhat big, challenge to try and translate the images of the characters that Eva had created into something visual, appealing and convincing. Who knows what yetis look like? That's what made this so exciting. My efforts went through many transitions as I attempted to create characters that were both obviously animal and yet also almost human. Their goodness, trust and high morality, as well as their vulnerability and quirkiness, were some of the qualities that I found endearing about them, and are ones that I've attempted to convey.

It has been an absolute dream to illustrate this book and I feel very privileged to have made this small contribution to such a wonderful story."

Read the opening chapter of

one
dog
and his
boy

Another classic animal adventure from Eva Ibbotson

1

Hal's Birthday

All Hal had ever wanted was a dog.

He had wanted one for his last birthday and for the birthday before, and for Christmas, and now that his birthday was coming round again he wanted one more desperately than ever. He had read about dogs and dreamed about dogs; he knew how to feed them and how to train them. But whenever he asked his mother for a dog she told him not to be silly.

"How could we have a dog? Think of the mess; hairs on the carpet and scratch marks on the door, and the smell. . . Not to mention puddles on the floor," said Albina Fenton, and shuddered.

And when Hal said that he would see to it that it didn't smell and would take it out again and again so that it didn't make puddles, she looked hurt.

"You have such a beautiful home," she told her son, "I would have thought you would be grateful."

This was true in a way. Hal's parents were rich; they lived in a large modern house in the suburbs with carpets so thick that your feet sank right into them and silk curtains that swept to the floor. There were three new cars in the garage – one for Albina, one for her husband and one for the maid to use when she took Hal to school – and five bathrooms with gold taps and power showers, and a sauna. In the kitchen every kind of gadget hummed and buzzed; squeezers and coffee makers and extractors – and the patio was tiled with marble brought in specially from Italy.

But in the whole of the house there was nothing that was alive. Not the smallest beetle, not the frailest spider, not the shyest mouse – Albina Fenton and the maids who came and went saw to that. And in the garden there were no flowers –

only raked gravel – because flowers mean earth and mess.

Although he knew it was silly to go on hoping, Hal decided he would have a last try. Three days before his tenth birthday he got up early and padded across the deep blue carpet, which was going to be replaced in the coming week because blue, his mother said, was out of fashion. He had said he liked blue but his mother had just smiled at him in that rather regretful way which meant that he had said something foolish.

Now he turned off his night light shaped like a flying saucer and wondered why he seemed to sleep just as badly with the flying saucer night light as he had done with the night light in the shape of a skyscraper.

Then he went into his bathroom and washed carefully, making sure that he didn't miss out any bits, and cleaned his teeth extra hard with his electric toothbrush before spraying his mouth with the high-pressure breath freshener fixed to the wall.

He wanted to have everything right before he wrote the note to his mother because it was important. If she took notice of it everything would come right, but if she didn't. . .

So now he sat down at his specially designed writing desk and found a pen and a piece of headed notepaper, because his parents hated anything to be scrappy, and wrote very, very carefully:

"PLEASE CAN I HAVE A DOG FOR MY BIRTHDAY? PLEASE?"

He wrote it out three times because he wanted the writing to be really good – his parents had moved him from his last school because they said he wasn't making enough progress – and then he padded across the corridor and pushed the note through his mother's bedroom door. There was no point in writing a note to his father because his father was in Dubai, or perhaps Hong Kong. Or even Tokyo. Hal could never be certain, though he tried very hard to keep track of his father's business travels. His father was a "frequent flyer" and more often in the air than on the ground.

Albina Fenton, Hal's mother, was in her walk-in wardrobe, trying to decide what to wear.

"Really, everything's in rags," she muttered, passing along a row of glittering evening dresses, then back along a line of tailored suits, opening drawers of frilly blouses and embroidered scarves. "I'll have to throw most of it away and start again. Some serious shopping is required."

When she came out of the wardrobe, she saw that someone had pushed a note under her door and her heart sank. It would be Hal. She hadn't forgotten his birthday; on the contrary, she had made all sorts of arrangements. She had ordered a gift pack from Hamleys and another from Harrods. They would pick out presents suitable for his age group and deliver them the day before and they had never failed her yet. A well-known caterer was bringing in the food and she had booked an entertainer for the party – but Hal had been difficult about the party because they had moved him from his old school to another one which was more suitable in every way, with the right kind of children, and for some reason Hal had been slow to make new friends.

She picked up the note. If only he isn't on about the same thing, she thought.

But he was, and now she had to explain to him again how impossible it was and had to endure it while Hal turned away and bit his lower lip and looked like a penniless orphan instead of a boy who had everything he could want in the world.

"It really isn't fair," she said to her friends when they came for morning coffee and Hal had been taken to his Activities Club by the maid. "I do everything for that boy and he is never thankful."

Her friends all had names which began with G: Glenda and Geraldine and Gloria – and they were quick to sympathize.

"But he does look a bit peaky," said Glenda. "I tell you what, I've read somewhere that they do kissograms for children on their birthdays. Or huggograms, I suppose they would be. They send someone dressed like a chimpanzee or some other animal, and he sings a funny song and delivers a message. Maybe they could get someone dressed like a dog?"

After her friends had gone, Albina rang her husband's office and asked his secretary to get a message through to him in Dubai. "Remind him that it's Hal's birthday on Friday," she said. "He'll be able to pick up a present for him in the Duty Free."

Really there wasn't any more she could do, thought Albina, and she picked up a furnishing catalogue from the pile on the coffee table. Everybody said that beige was the "in" colour this year; she'd have to get rid of the white carpet in the dining room. . . Not that they'd be here much longer: she really felt quite shamed living in a house without a swimming pool.

Right up to the last minute, Hal went on hoping.

He would open his eyes on the morning of his

birthday and hear a snuffling noise outside the door and the dog would come running in . . . sometimes the dog was brown and fluffy, sometimes it was white with a smooth coat. Hal didn't mind what it looked like; it would be alive, and it would belong to him, and it would be there when his father was in Dubai and his mother was out with her friends and he was alone in the house with the maid who changed every month and was always so homesick and so sad.

But the phantom dog remained a phantom. Nobody scratched on the door when Hal's birthday came and the sound of barking which made Hal's heart beat fast turned out to be in the street. Hal dressed and went downstairs, where his mother waited beside the breakfast table piled high with parcels. Hamleys was not the best known toy shop in London for nothing; they had sent the latest Xbox game, and a new board game and a laser gun and a radio-controlled metal-detecting car. Harrods had sent an iPod and a giant chemistry set and a Roboquad. . .

"Now are you happy?" said his mother, watching him as he opened his parcels, and he said yes, he was, and she told him that his father would be back that evening and would bring something from the airport.

"Did my grandparents send me anything?" asked Hal, and Albina sighed and produced a small packet wrapped in brown paper.

Her husband's parents were poor and lived in a small cottage on the Northumbrian coast. They had come on a visit once when Hal was small, carrying their belongings in an ancient suitcase tied up with string – and really it had been impossible not to be ashamed of them. They hadn't come again, but they sent the most extraordinary gifts for Hal at Christmas and on his birthday. If one couldn't afford a proper present, surely it was better to do nothing than send a seashell or a piece of rock, thought Albina. Yet Hal always looked pleased with their gifts, and now he gazed at something small and brown and crumbly as he had not looked at any of his other things.

"It's a sea horse," he said, looking at the note that came with it. "It got washed up on one of the rocks. The fishermen say that it brings luck."

So Hal took his presents upstairs and played with them, and in the afternoon the van arrived with the party tea and the birthday cake shaped like a pair of trainers (because nothing that Albina ordered was shaped like itself, and a cake that looked like a cake would have bored her very much). Then the friends came – only they weren't really his friends; he had left those at his old school – and played with his toys and broke the metal-detecting car and tipped the chemistry set on the floor.

But after they had had tea and watched a conjurer there came a surprise.

A van drew up outside; the bell rang – and then the door opened and a . . . thing . . . burst into the room. It was big and dressed in a yellow furry skin, and it had floppy black ears, a lolling pink tongue, and a tail.

For a moment it pranced about on two legs; then it dropped down on all fours and crawled towards Hal and an odd strangled noise came from it which sounded like "Woof, woof."

When it reached Hal, it dropped a big greeting card from its mouth – and in a hoarse voice it began to sing.

"I am your Birthday Doggie,

Your Doggie for the day.

Just pat me and I'll—"

But the song broke off with a splutter because Hal had gone mad.

"Stop it. Come out of there," he yelled, pulling at the creature's head. "How dare you?" He gave a last tug, and the sweaty red face of the man from the Huggograms Agency stared at him. "How dare you pretend to be a dog!" And he began to kick at the man's shins. "You're disgusting. Get out. Go away."

But Alfred Potts, the man inside the suit, had worked hard at his routine. He hadn't had a fag for a whole hour, and he'd cut down on the beer before he came, and he wasn't going to be kicked by a flea-sized kid.

"Now you just pipe down, will you," he said, gripping Hal's arm. "Here's your mum trying to give you a bit of fun, you ungrateful little—"

But before he could finish, Hal slipped from his grasp and ran sobbing out of the room.

And that was the end of the party.